THE PLAY OF *His Life*

· · · · · · · · · · · ·

AMY AISLIN

PRAISE FOR

"*Shots on Goal* is a strong addition to Aislin's delicious world-building surrounding the sexy, competitive world of hockey."—*Shots on Goal*
LUCY LENNOX, BESTSELLING AUTHOR

"With lots of hockey, delicious food, and the sweetest couple ever, Amy Aislin scores a hat trick with *Shots on Goal.*"—*Shots on Goal*
KELLY JENSEN, AWARD-WINNING AUTHOR OF BLOCK AND STRIKE

"I'm a sucker for a well-written second-chance romance and that's exactly what we get with Amy Aislin's second novel in her Stick Side series."—*The Nature of the Game*
DOG-EARED DAYDREAMS

"I'm still floored by this book. It's well-written, atmospheric, often funny, often heartbreaking, and devastatingly romantic."—*On the Ice*
LOVE BYTES REVIEWS

"This small town Christmas romance is full of festive cheer."—*Christmas Lane*
WICKED READS

"I LOVED Nat and Quinn so much, and am so impressed with the story that Amy Aislin wove together here. I enjoyed this one a TON."—*The Heights*
THE NOVEL APPROACH REVIEWS

ALSO BY

STICK SIDE SERIES
On the Ice
The Nature of the Game
Shots on Goal
Risking the Shot

WINDSOR, WYOMING SERIES
Home for a Cowboy

LIGHTHOUSE BAY SERIES
Christmas Lane
Gingerbread Mistletoe

LAKESHORE SERIES
The Heights

OTHER BOOKS
Ballerina Dad
Elias
As Big as the Sky

For Mom and Dad. Because you've always encouraged me to follow my dreams. A girl couldn't ask for better parents.

CHAPTER
One

Now serving alcohol?

Christian Dufresne read the sign again and then a third time. But no. The words didn't magically reconfigure themselves into something more likely, like *Now serving apple turnovers! Or Now serving paninis! Or Now serving the best crepes in town...with REAL maple syrup!*

Not that Christian had ever had their crepes—this place hadn't existed the last time he came to town—but they looked awesome in the picture on the display board he could see through the glass window. He'd reserve judgement on their worthiness after he found out whether or not they offered real maple syrup, or just the gross, generic, gloopy kind found in grocery stores everywhere except Quebec and Vermont.

If it wasn't real, it wasn't worth it.

And look at that. He'd just made up a new slogan for real maple syrup! He should be in marketing. Oh wait. He was!

But seriously. What the hell was the point of a small bakery that didn't even serve dinner—they closed at five, for the love of God—offering alcohol? Did nine-to-fivers working in downtown Oakville order a glass of wine or beer to enjoy with their muffin or mini quiche or cookie or lemon tart? Were they that bored with life in suburbia?

Or maybe just that desperate.

The door handle turned easily in his hand and he stepped inside, out of the blowing snow and into the heated bakery. He took his gloves off and felt his fingers start to thaw. Goddamn the fucking snow. Actually, no. Scratch that. Goddamn the *cold*. A windchill of minus twenty degrees

Celsius just made him want to lie in the street and die. Game over. The only good thing about winter? Hockey. And snowboarding. But mostly hockey.

It was empty inside the bakery, a surprise given the amount of people out on the street no doubt doing some last minute Christmas shopping. Why they didn't head to an indoor mall—they were heated!—was beyond him. Instead they went in and out of stores on Lakeshore Road like it wasn't cold enough to freeze your boogers.

Idiots. All of them.

Although he could probably be lumped into that category as well, couldn't he? He'd been walking outside too as if living in Vancouver hadn't desensitized him to this kind of bone-deep cold. All because his mother wanted a fresh baguette from the new bakery, Warm Glow, to go with dinner. He'd barely stepped foot in the house before she was already sending him on an errand. Seriously, he hadn't even brought his duffle bag to his old room yet.

Outside, the wind blew so strong it rattled the door and dislodged a clump of snow from the bakery's awning. It fell to the sidewalk with a crunchy-sounding *splat*, narrowly missing a woman laden with shopping bags. This. This was why he lived in Vancouver. Mild winters and little snow.

Goddamn Ontario winters.

All that effort and it looked like his mother wasn't going to get her bread after all. Inside the bakery a store employee wearing a green apron was upending chairs and setting them on the tables upside down.

Crap. He looked behind him, and sure enough a sign on the front door's glass window read *Open*. Which meant the *Closed* side faced the street he'd just come from. Whoops. Well, the door had been unlocked.

Christian went to inform the employee that he'd forgotten to lock the door but something...something in the way the guy moved...how he didn't favor his right knee so much as paid attention to how and where he stepped. How his spiked dark blond hair reflected the light from the ceiling lamps. How the muscles in those broad shoulders moved under his T-shirt. How tight that butt looked in those dark jeans.

A hot rush of familiarity swept through him and wings grew in his stomach. And then he brilliantly said, "You!"

The employee turned quickly, knocking an elbow into one of the chairs on the table next to him. It crashed into another, and the resulting clatter when they hit the floor acted like a goal horn going off in Christian's head. Jolting into action, he rushed forward and tried to save a third chair. But the other guy already had it and Christian's hold on it only served to unbalance them both. They played an accidental tug-of-war as they desperately tried to right themselves, but either one of them slipped, or the floor decided to move, or unseen hands pushed them. Whatever the reason, the two humans in the room joined the chairs on the floor.

Goddamn fucking fresh bread. Goddamn his mother's innocent, "The new bakery on Lakeshore has the best Italian baguette. Could you go grab one for me? We need it for dinner." And goddamn the idiot underneath him who was laughing his fool head off.

"Are you kidding me?" Christian grumbled, trying to take stock of what, if anything, hurt. It only made the tool on the floor laugh harder.

And goddamn tall, jacked, blue-eyed, blond ex-boyfriends too while he was at it.

But that laugh. It hit him right in the solar plexus, right where he kept their memories tightly buried so they didn't incapacitate him when he wasn't looking.

That laugh was instant friendship. It was two new French Canadian seven-year-olds making fast friends in school when they realized they could have a conversation in a language no one else could understand. It was summer days spent riding their bikes to the corner store. It was winters snowboarding and playing hockey. It was Christmases sneaking into each other's windows. It was starting high school thinking they'd be best friends forever. It was that first kiss in tenth grade, and the second one only seconds after, and the very last one years later, at a time when they had needed each other more than ever.

It was home.

Blinking against the onslaught of never-forgotten memories, Christian groaned and sat up, taking care to touch Riley as little as possible as he did so. Even though what he really wanted was to spread himself out all over him.

Don't think about the guy underneath you. On his back. Looking hotter than ever. Nope. Don't go there. No dirty thoughts here.

"Fucking ghosts," he said instead.

Riley was crying tears of laughter.

"What the fuck is so funny?" Christian asked.

"You," Riley said when he could breathe again. "You're still Crotchety Christian."

"Fuck you," Christian said, and hauled himself off the floor.

Once upon a time a "Fuck you" from one of them would have resulted in a "Sure. How do you want me?" from the other. Which, more often than not, led to much more pleasurable activities. But it'd been six years since the last...

...Since the last.

"You're still blaming ghosts for everything." Riley interrupted his thoughts.

"Fucking Ouija board," Christian muttered.

"Dude, it was fifteen years ago," Riley pointed out unhelpfully. He sat up, then used the table to haul himself to standing. Shit. Had their fall further messed up Riley's knee? But no. Once upright, Riley stretched out his knee, tested his weight on it, then bent with ease to pick up the fallen chairs. His biceps flexed under the short sleeves of his T-shirt and Christian didn't bother fighting the memory of how they'd once felt under his hands, his mouth. He felt the flush overtake his cheeks and reach his ears. Hopefully Riley would think it was a result of their recent...exertions.

"Well, in fifteen years I haven't figured out how to out-Ouija them and send them back to where they came from," Christian said. "Have you?"

"Nope." Riley laughed a little and grinned at Christian like he was having the best day ever. Damn but Christian had missed Riley's constant optimism and good humor.

"Well, there you go," Christian said. Like that was that.

Riley snorted. "That makes no sense at all."

Finished with placing the chairs back on the tables—with no help from Christian. No, he was too busy ogling Riley's ass as he bent and stood, bent and stood. Jesus, could he be more obvious?—Riley turned those ocean eyes on him and his goofy, happy grin shifted from hi-old-friend-I-haven't-seen-in-a-while to hi-ex-lover-I-never-got-over.

Or maybe Christian was projecting.

And before Christian could say "Can we go back to the way things were?" or "God, I missed you," or "Please take me home and never let me go again," or "RILEY, I STILL LOVE YOU!", Riley reached out and yanked Christian hard against him. Not to kiss him. Or to throw him down on the nearest available surface and have his glorious way with him. No, clearly it was only Christian who was having an X-rated party in his head.

Those arms he'd been admiring earlier wrapped around him in a hug and Christian reacted on instinct, wrapping his own around Riley and hanging on tight. Riley had always meant home and belonging and safety. That feeling hadn't changed and it left Christian wondering why the hell they'd ever broken up in the first place.

Ignoring the old hurt Riley's presence dredged up, Christian buried his nose in Riley's neck, an easy feat since they were evenly matched in height. He inhaled deeply and smelled pastry and sweat and Riley's familiar spiciness.

"Hi," Riley whispered in his ear.

Christian had to swallow past the growing knot in his throat. Stupid emotions. "Hi."

"Want a drink?"

"Oh, fuck yes."

They released each other before things got awkward. And avoided eye contact because okay, maybe things were already a little awkward.

Riley headed for the counter with nary a limp to be seen. A hockey injury two years ago had damaged his knee and ended his pro career. What had been devastating for Christian was probably a hundred times more so for Riley. But looking at Riley now as he moved around behind the counter, a slight smile on his face, knee fully recuperated, he looked as healthy and happy as ever.

For Christian, Riley's injury had been a huge WTF moment. A nodus tollens, if you will, which was basically a fancy word for "how the hell is this my life right now?"

A hockey scholarship had taken Riley to the University of Denver right after high school graduation. Christian headed west to the University of British Columbia—or UBC as the locals called it. They'd gone from seeing each other every day for ten years, to seeing each other once every few weeks. Result? The eventual end of their relationship. And when Riley had been injured it had seemed like all of the loneliness, all of the pain, all of the heartbreak of being apart and then *being apart* had been for nothing.

Christian stared hard at one of the ceiling lamps, letting

the light burn the wetness out of his eyes. If he didn't stop thinking about what could've been he was going to curl up in a corner of Warm Glow and sob his sad heart out.

Distracting himself, he studied the bakery. It was rustic, like something found in the middle of Cottage Country. Low-hanging ceiling lamps, distressed wood tables and chairs, wood-paneled floors. A long display case was currently free of food and held only empty baskets. The digital display board above the counter listed menu items presumably not found in the display case, including those mouth-watering crepes. Next to the front door, a long, high table was tucked against the window with tall stools underneath. The place was decked out for Christmas: a wreath on the door, garlands on the walls, lights in the window, festive candles on all the tables.

Christian locked the front door. When he turned back, it was to find Riley standing behind the counter, operating a machine and making...hot chocolate? Well damn. Not that he didn't love a good hot chocolate but when Riley had suggested a drink Christian had thought he'd be getting something that would dull his senses.

Riley raised an eyebrow and nodded at the front door.

"Your closed sign is up, but your door wasn't locked," Christian explained.

Riley grunted and poured the drink into a couple of mugs. "I'm always doing that. Your mother's constantly on my case about it."

His mother. Who had sent him on this errand. Did she even want fresh bread? Unlikely. Was she at home making dinner? Definitely not. She was probably at her BFF's down the street, cackling at how she'd so easily fooled her clueless son. Sending him on this "errand," knowing exactly who he'd run into. They were going to have words later, that was for damn sure.

"I thought you were giving me booze," Christian said.

Riley merely turned and grabbed a brown bottle off a shelf behind him. Tall and thin, it had a yellow label and the words *Kahlùa* splashed on the front in bold, red letters. Riley yanked out the stopper and poured a generous amount into both mugs.

Christian perked up. Spiked hot chocolate. Was there anything better?

Sex with Riley.

Quit it, brain!

Riley set one of the mugs closer to Christian, picked up his own, clinked it against Christian's and said, "Cheers." Then he took a healthy swallow, ocean eyes never leaving Christian's.

Yeah, Christian knew a dare when he saw one. Determined not be outdone, he raised his mug in a silent toast and took a large gulp.

"So?" Riley said.

"It's good. Rich."

"Yeah. Thought you'd like that. Unless you've lost the taste for hot chocolate over the past six years."

The reminder of how long it'd been since they'd seen each other brought a halt to their conversation. Christian looked away from Riley and fiddled with the label on the bottle. The weird mix of apprehensiveness, hopefulness, and happiness combined with the alcohol in his belly was making him feel... surprisingly mellow.

He cleared his throat. "The chocolate's really good." It was almost bittersweet but not quite, sitting thick on his tongue. It was magic in his mouth. "What kind do you use?"

"I can't give away all my secrets," Riley said with a wink.

Whatever. Christian couldn't bring himself to care anymore. The Mysterious Case of the Delicious Hot Chocolate would have to wait another day. His drink was awesome and that was all that mattered.

And Riley. Riley definitely mattered. Christian was feeling so relaxed all he wanted to do was crawl into bed and cuddle with his boyfriend forever.

Ex-boyfriend. Who he smiled at like a dope with his first crush.

Man, maybe he should've eaten more than the pretzels on the flight over. Two sips and he was already at that stage of buzzed that made him sleepy. The one that came right before being drunk off his ass and unable to walk.

Although, in his defense, Riley was grinning stupidly at him, too. The wings in his stomach turned dragon-sized. The only times he'd ever felt this strange feeling of anxious excitement also had to do with Riley. Their first kiss. Graduating from hand jobs to blowjobs. The first time they had sex.

The last time. The last time that Christian had thought meant so much. Only to wake up the next morning to find Riley gone.

"How long are you in town for?" Riley asked, and he sounded as drugged as Christian felt.

"Just until..." *Boxing Day*, he almost said. But that was only five days away. Not enough time to get his Riley-fix. What if they could get the friendship back that they'd once had? The fact that Christian was still in love with Riley after all these years probably meant he was pretty pathetic.

But the truth was that he missed his best friend just as much as he missed his boyfriend.

He cleared his throat. "Until after the new year."

And now he had to make some phone calls. First to his boss about taking the extra time off. Second to the airline, which would probably charge him as much as his plane ticket to reschedule his flight.

Given the soft smile on Riley's face, it'd be completely worth it.

"You don't need your cane anymore?" Christian asked.

The look on Riley's face could only be described as surprised pleasure. Because Christian couldn't keep his mouth shut and had given himself away.

Yes, he still cared. So sue him.

He cleared his throat. "I, uh...followed your career. You know? Obviously." He was sure his shrug made him look like he was having a seizure. Forcing his shaking hands not to betray him, he brought his mug up to his mouth for another sip. "I'm sorry that happened to you, Riles."

Riley only grunted. "I knew the risks of playing pro sports. Besides, I was told I was lucky. The way I fell the injury should've been a lot worse. As in a knee brace and a cane for the rest of my life, but..." He held both hands up like, *cane-free, bitches!*

"I thought you would've—" *called me.* Um, no. No, no. *Things not to say to your ex who doesn't seem to be nearly as affected by your reappearance in his life as you are by his.* "Gone into coaching," Christian finally went with.

"I thought about it," Riley admitted. "But after I got hurt, I just...needed a bit of distance from hockey."

"So you decided to work in a bakery?"

"No," Riley said. "I decided to start my own." His voice held a tinge of disbelief, like he couldn't quite believe he'd gone ahead and *started a bakery*. Who did that anyway?

"You started a bakery," Christian repeated slowly, trying and failing to keep the incredulousness out of his tone, "in downtown Oakville. Where the rent prices are notoriously insane?" Businesses opened and folded so fast Christian couldn't keep up. The only ones that stayed open were the ones that had been established for years.

"Yeah." Riley looked away as if this was a subject he didn't want to talk about.

Christian ignored it and plowed forward anyway. "Are you having trouble?"

Riley waved his hand, physically brushing the topic aside. "I'm fine," he said with a smile that was so patently forced.

And that hurt, that Riley wouldn't confide in him. They used to tell each other everything. But what did he expect after six years of radio silence?

Finishing off his hot chocolate, Christian set his mug down and forced a smile of his own. "I should get going. I'm sure you have stuff to do. Thanks for the hot chocolate." He eyed the Kahlùa bottle on the shelf behind the counter. "And the booze."

Riley chuckled. "You're welcome. Hey, don't be a stranger, okay? I'm here almost every day. Come by for lunch when you have a free afternoon?"

Christian would be here for lunch every afternoon if that wouldn't make him look like a psycho stalker on crack.

"I will," he promised. The questions he wanted to ask burned a hole in his gut, but he left them unasked. Instead he took a good look at Riley. Because though he was almost certain this wasn't the last time they'd see each other, he'd thought the same six years ago. And look how that had turned out. So he looked his fill, not caring that his feelings were probably on full display. Because who cared about looking like a vulnerable sap when you'd spent the past six years missing your best friend? Some things were more important than pride.

Rapping his knuckles twice on the countertop in a silent goodbye, Christian turned to leave. Wishing he had the guts to tell Riley everything he wanted from him. Wishing—

"Hey, T?"

Breath left him in a whoosh at the nickname. The one

Riley had started called him from the day they'd met for some inexplicable reason Riley had never ever divulged. None of Christian's names started with a T, so where Riley had gotten it from Christian might never know. Its utterance now made him think maybe Riley wasn't as unaffected by their sudden reunion as he'd thought.

Christian turned to Riley, who had come around the counter and now stood only a couple feet away. Unfamiliar shadows danced in his eyes.

"What are you doing on Sunday?" Riley asked.

"It's Christmas Eve."

Riley smiled at the nonanswer. "That doesn't answer my question."

Christian shrugged. "Having dinner with my mom." Same as every Christmas Eve.

"We close at two that day," Riley said. "Want to hit the ice after?"

Hell yeah, did he ever! He was sure his answering smile held a faint hint of relief as they worked out the details of when and where.

"Bring your gear!" Riley called to him after he'd unlocked the front door to let himself out.

"For a friendly game?"

"Dude, you forget. I've seen your slap shot. No way am I getting in net without padding."

Damn, did he even have any gear at his mom's anymore? Whatever. He'd find something.

Waving a hand over his shoulder to acknowledge he'd heard, Christian let himself out, said "Don't forget to lock this before you leave!" waited for the "Yeah, yeah" from inside, and shut the door behind him.

CHAPTER
Two

Riley Deschamps counted to ten in his head and then bounded across his shop in two steps. Plastering his cheek against the cold front window, he squinted into the darkness for a last glimpse of Christian. That might be him at the stop sign, waiting for cars to pass before he crossed. It was hard to tell in the dark.

Resisting the urge to chase after him, Riley watched maybe-Christian cross the road and disappear down a side street.

He didn't realize his hands were shaking until he started washing the mugs.

Christian Dufresne. How was it possible to think you remembered what a person looked like only to be dead wrong? Christian's icy blue eyes were more intense than Riley remembered, his hair was darker, his cheekbones sharper, his brows bolder, lips poutier. And that darker-than-a-five-o'clock-shadow-yet-not-quite-a-full-beard beard...that was new. For as long as Riley had known him Christian had always been clean-shaven. But holy moly, the beard was hot. Made him want to reach out and trace it with his fingertips.

Riley was pretty sure Christian would let him. The man had never been any good at hiding his emotions and truthfully? He'd never seemed to care to. Especially when it came to Riley.

If it weren't for Christian, they never would've been anything past best friends. One Saturday afternoon in October of grade ten, on their walk home from hockey practice, Christian had interrupted Riley's tirade about a school classmate who wasn't pulling his weight on a group project and planted one on him, right there on the sidewalk, in front of God and any unfortunate pedestrians.

Brave. But also so stupid.

Riley had been so freaked. So thankful, too, because fuck did he have a crush on his best friend with no idea what to do about it.

But it had been all Christian. Christian who initiated that first kiss, then the next one right afte —the one that had convinced Riley not to run away from his feelings. Because that second kiss meant that the first one hadn't been a fluke. It had been Christian who initiated their first make-out session, their first official date, the boyfriend talk, their first hand jobs, first blowjobs, the sex talk, *sex*.

And Riley had gone along willingly. A million percent willingly. Because Christian was...Christian was everything.

Was still everything, as it turned out.

It was a bit of a kick to the ass to realize he wasn't as over Christian as he'd thought.

As in, not at all. Great.

The good news was that Christian didn't appear to hate him. After the way Riley had left things after they'd hooked up six years ago—because no one in their right mind, after a night of better-than-spectacular sex, thought disappearing before the sun came up a good thing—he hadn't expected Christian to ever again look at him the way he had today: with warmth and happiness and okay, a touch of that familiar grouchiness, too.

But man, that had been a shit time. Riley finished closing up, bundled into his many layers, locked up behind him, and started his short walk home in minus twenty-degree weather, following the same path maybe-Christian had taken only a half hour earlier.

Downtown Oakville, and this section of Lakeshore Road in

particular between Navy and Allan Streets, always reminded him of Los Olas Boulevard in Fort Lauderdale. Small shops interspersed with restaurants, bakeries, ice cream parlors, and hair salons. But without the island in the middle of the street. And it wasn't surrounded with tall buildings—Oakville had some kind of bylaw that prevented buildings from being above a certain height. And without palm trees, because this was Canada and the only palm trees in Canada were...well, nowhere.

The further he walked from downtown, heading south toward Lake Ontario, the quieter it got as he entered the residential area with its old, historic homes. He could hear the waves lapping against the shore. He'd grown up hearing that sound outside his bedroom window and hadn't realized he'd missed it until he moved back home for good after he injured his knee a couple years ago. The injury had been so bad it had cut his pro hockey career short after only just three years. But those years had been awesome and he never looked back on them with what-ifs or regrets.

Speaking of regrets...

Rewind seven and a half years, to the end of their second year at university. When Riley had decided to stay in Colorado over the summer to go to an exclusive hockey training camp he'd been chosen to attend. Instead of coming home like he'd promised. Where Christian already had a summer internship lined up in Toronto—only half an hour east of Oakville—and was just waiting for Riley to come join him for a few weeks.

But Riley hadn't. And Christian couldn't do it anymore. The separation was killing him; Riley could see it happen, even over Skype's pixelated connection. Christian was hardwired to shower affection on the people he loved. He needed to see Riley, to touch him and hear him and smell him for longer than the brief periods they'd managed to get together between their classes and midterms and exams and part-time jobs and Riley's hockey games and practices.

And Riley had understood. So he hadn't fought for them. Even though it felt like his heart was being cut out of his chest with a rusty spoon.

In hindsight, that was his biggest regret. It had cost him his best friend.

But he couldn't regret staying in Colorado for hockey camp. He credited it with making him a better player, which had eventually led to being a first-round NHL draft pick.

He just wished things could've been different.

Fast forward almost a year and a half after their breakup, to the start of their fourth year. Christian's dad passed away of a stroke unexpectedly. And Riley couldn't *not* go to the funeral. Christian's parents, Sylvie and Charles, had been a second set of parents to Riley growing up. And Christian had been a mess.

Granted, sleeping with Christian the night after the funeral probably hadn't been smart. But Christian had been so sad, and he'd seemed so alone. Riley had known it was a mistake afterward, as they'd lain in bed talking and Riley had realized that Christian was subtly dropping hints about moving to Denver to be with Riley, despite still having two semesters left of school.

And Riley had panicked. He hadn't wanted to be a person someone else gave up everything for. So he'd left as soon as Christian fell asleep.

Fine, *that* was his biggest regret. Not staying. Not trying. Not keeping in touch. But it was too late now.

Or was it?

His extremities were numb and his right knee twinged by the time he reached the driveway of his clapboard house on Front Street. Riley looked northeast, in the direction of Christian's house on King Street, where Christian's mom still lived and where Christian probably was right now. Less than a five-minute walk away. He remembered the way Christian had tucked his face in Riley's neck when they'd hugged earlier, just like he used to. And his choked voice when he'd said hi. And how he'd looked so reluctant to leave the bakery. And the delighted smile when Riley had suggested a hockey game.

All was obviously not lost. It was an opportunity he wasn't going to pass up again.

OF COURSE, CHRISTIAN SHOWED UP AT WARM GLOW THE next day in the middle of the craziest of lunch hours.

Fine, to be fair, Riley had told him to come for lunch, but in his defense, Riley hadn't expected the Friday before the Christmas weekend to be this insane. It was like everyone who worked and shopped downtown Oakville forgot there were other restaurants and bakeries on Lakeshore to lunch at.

Yeah, okay, maybe he was just frustrated that one of his part-timers "forgot" she had a final exam today and couldn't come in for her lunchtime shift. Christian walked in, took one look at the lineup Riley was serving, another at the tables Riley hadn't had time to clear. Then he came around the counter and disappeared into the kitchen. Riley barely had time to wonder what the hell he was doing before he came back out with a large bin and started clearing tables.

The relief Riley felt was overwhelming. One wrong move and someone would post a negative review on Yelp or Urban Spoon or whatever app the kids were using these days to avoid making decisions. And his little bakery couldn't afford the bad press until it was a little more established. It was already hard enough making rent every month. They didn't need to lose any customers.

He lost track of Christian while he took orders but he was

always peripherally aware of him coming and going from the kitchen. Riley could hear Samantha, his business partner and Warm Glow's live-in baker and cook—literally. She lived above the shop—talking in the kitchen, which meant she'd made Christian's acquaintance. When he screwed up an order because he was busy thinking about trying not to think about Christian, Riley pretended this day was the same as any other and that Christian was still in Vancouver and went about his business.

Christian's gruff laughter from the back shot that plan to hell.

It was almost an hour later that the line disappeared, though a few people remained at the tables.

"Is it just me, or was that busier than normal?" his other part-timer, Henry, asked. Henry was a seventy-year-old retired army vet who only worked Tuesdays and Fridays because those were the days his wife hosted her knitting club and it was either get the hell out of the house or listen to them talk about the misadventures of their various grandkids.

"Everything's crazier at the holidays," Riley replied, wiping down the drinks counter.

Henry started wiping down the small counter that held the condiments. "Should've seen the fight that broke out over a parking spot at the Toys "R" Us yesterday. Thought I was going to have to use my army general's voice."

Riley had heard Henry's army general voice. It was terrifying.

Speaking of terrifying voices, where was Christian? Not that his voice was terrifying, but his grumpiness had been known to scare a kid or two.

Riley turned and there Christian was, standing in the doorway to the kitchen, hands on his hips. He wore one of Warm Glow's green aprons over jeans and a dark blue T-shirt. Just the sight of him made Riley's heart flip.

Christian had always been a big guy, but Riley had forgotten just how imposing he could be when he scowled that way. And what was with his pouf hairstyle? A pompadour, was it? Riley had seen hairstyles like that on guys before and thought those men should be on the cover of cheesy romance novels. But Christian pulled it off, probably because he could scowl anybody into liking anything.

"Is it my turn to order now?" Christian asked.

It made Riley laugh and the tension drained from his shoulders. "Sure, what do you want?"

"What's good?"

"Seriously? You're asking me that in my own bakery? Everything's good. The salad—"

"What guy likes *salad?*" Christian interrupted. He said "salad" like "peas"—which Riley knew Christian hated more than any food ever.

"I like salad," Riley said, slightly offended. Warm Glow's salads were good, damn it!

"Me, too," Henry said, coming around the counter to grab a wet cloth. "Know why?"

"Because you're turning over a new leaf?" Christian suggested.

Riley just looked at him.

"What?" Christian said. "That was funny."

"That was as lame as ever."

"I thought it was funny," Henry said.

"Me, too," piped in a customer adding milk to his coffee.

Christian raised an eyebrow at Riley like, *see?*

"Awww," Riley gushed. "You have fans."

That got Christian scowling again.

"Thanks for your help at the shop," Riley said, breath puffing out in front of him in a white cloud.

He'd sent both Sam and Henry on lunch breaks after the busy rush and now, an hour later, he was finally taking his own. Walking along Lakeshore in the middle of a Friday after-noon with Christian was surreal and yet...not. They fell into a rhythm that belied yesterday's brief moment of awkwardness. Christian slurped his tea the same way he always had. The familiarity made Riley's heart ache for the lost years between them.

At the bottom of Navy Street was Lakeside Park. Ignoring the empty jungle gym, they headed along the path and, as if by mutual agreement, took a seat at their favorite bench that overlooked the lake. The day was grey and overcast and it was at least five degrees colder next to the water. The leafless trees creaked in the wind.

Riley huddled in his winter coat, bringing his scarf up over his mouth and nose. It was really too cold to be sitting outside, but it was nice to get out of the shop for a little while. And it was doubly nice to have company. Especially the Christian kind.

Christian sat with one ankle crossed over the other knee, sipping occasionally from his cup. The way he looked at the lake as if not quite seeing it, one arm braced against the back of the bench, sent a hot rush of familiarity through Riley. Riley kept using that word, but it was the only one he could think of to explain this sense of rightness at having Christian back in his life. Even the easy silence between them was familiar, not piled high with remorse or tension or unforgive-ness like Riley would've thought.

It was like they'd automatically reverted to who they'd been together years ago. Just without the sex. It made Riley grin into his scarf.

Christian sighed. "I missed this."

Riley didn't have the guts to ask what he meant by *this*. The cold? Their bench? Being together?

"Miss the sound."

Ah. He was talking about the lake.

"Not enough water in Vancouver for you?" Riley joked.

"I saw whales once," Christian said. "Killer whales."

"You did not."

"Did, too. A whole pack of them. Saw them out of my office window."

That sounded awesome to Riley. "And you miss *this*?" He waved at the water in front of them. "A nasty lake with what's probably some really nasty fish in it?"

"This lake has a lot of shipwrecks in it."

Had Riley not spent as much time as he had with Christian growing up, Christian's seeming changes in conversations might've made his head spin. As it was he knew that "This lake has a lot of shipwrecks in it" was Christian-speak for, "The Pacific Ocean might have cool creatures, but this is where I grew up and this is *my* lake and I miss home." It made Riley smile fondly at him. But he chickened out at the last minute and didn't ask Christian why he didn't move back if he missed home so much.

"You would know something like that," he said instead.

"I also know that Warm Glow is a stupid name for a bakery," Christian said. "Sounds like the name of a specialty tea shop. Or a salon."

Riley couldn't help his snorted laugh. "You have as much tact as ever."

"Tact never got anybody anywhere."

That was arguable but Riley was having too good an afternoon to debate the topic.

He didn't realize he was shivering uncontrollably until Christian said, "Come on. Let's walk before you freeze to death."

Riley wasn't ready yet for his lunch break to end, so he was grateful when Christian led them not back up Navy, but east along the gravel path that followed the lake. And he was doubly grateful when Christian handed over his tea without a word. He took a sip and sighed in bliss as he was warmed from the inside.

"How long have you had Warm Glow?"

Riley had to force his attention off how close Christian was, how hot that stupid hairstyle looked, how damn sexy that dark not-quite-a-beard was. It brought out his icy blue eyes. "Since the beginning of October," he said, distracting himself from Christian's nearness. "Sam's husband and I played for Toronto at the same time. She'd always wanted her own bakery, but she didn't want the deal-with-the-people part, you know? She just wanted to bake and cook. We spent a lot of time together after I got hurt and she talked about it a lot. I needed something to do after hockey and I figured this was something we could do together. She could make the food and I'd deal with the front."

They turned left on Thomas Street to head back up to Lakeshore. Christian bumped his shoulder against Riley's.

"That's nice that you did that for her," he said, and Riley couldn't help but notice—not for the first time—how good Christian smelled. "But is it what you wanted?"

"I like it," Riley said. And even to his own ears it didn't sound convincing. "It was something I needed at the time. Like I said yesterday, I needed to distance myself from hockey for a bit. And I actually like working the front. I meet a lot of people that way."

"You've always been a people person," Christian said.

They reached Lakeshore and, "Hey Riley!" someone shouted from across the street. Another greeting came from their left. Christian's smug smile wasn't lost on Riley.

"Local boy makes it big in the pros?" he said.

Riley huffed a laugh. "More like, local boy makes it big in the pros and then comes back home to contribute to the local economy."

Christian's gruff laugh reached right into Riley's belly and warmed him up even more effectively than the tea. If they could have more days like this before Christian went back to Vancouver after the new year, maybe Riley wouldn't have to live without his best friend for the rest of his life.

CHAPTER
Three

IN THE MIDDLE OF THEIR NEIGHBORHOOD, ABOUT HALFWAY between their houses, was a small pond that froze over every winter. Riley was already there when Christian arrived at three o'clock on Christmas Eve, lugging his very, very old hockey gear and a tiny dog.

"Trevor!" The dog took off at Riley's greeting, making a beeline for him. Already wearing his gear, Riley couldn't crouch to greet the little shih tzu, so he bent at the waist and gave the dog a pat on the head.

Christian stopped at the edge of the pond and admired the way Riley's jeans molded to his deliciously tight ass. Riley may not play in the pros anymore, but he still had an incredible goalie butt.

"I see you two know each other," Christian said, mildly offended at the dog's abandonment. Trevor clearly preferred Riley over Christian.

"Your mom brings him into the shop all the time."

Christian grimaced. "You still see my mom?" Riley had mentioned something of the sort the other day, too.

"All the time. I see her more than I see you."

Riley stiffened for a second as he seemed to realize what he'd said. Christian stood looking at him, unimpressed. Because really, who was it that ran out after they'd hooked up the last time, after his dad's funeral?

Riley gave him a tight smile that said something like, *Yeah, well, the phone works both ways, dude.*

Impasse.

They'd have to talk about it sometime, but today wasn't that day.

"You gonna stand there all day," Riley said, "or are we gonna play?"

The mirth in his eyes told Christian that yes, Riley was aware of the double entendre he'd just uttered.

Oh, they were going to play, all right.

They didn't bother with skates; the frozen pond was too bumpy for it to be safe. But Riley had brought his old hockey net, so at least they had a real goal.

Christian put on his gear—it was a bit of a tight fit, but it'd do—grabbed his hockey stick and a puck and moved to center ice.

"Trevor," Christian said, and pointed with his stick. Trevor moved off the ice to nose at some dead plants poking through the snow against a fence.

"Think you'll finally get one past me?" Riley asked, pulling on his mask. Christian would not call that smirk sexy no matter how much it made his blood sing.

"Finally? You must be forgetting all the previous times I scored on you."

Now there he went with the double entendres.

"Ha! If by 'all' you mean 'never.' Bring it, Dufresne. Bet you can't get one past me."

"Bet? Okay." Christian nodded once decisively. "If I get one past you, you tell me where you get your delicious magic chocolate from."

Riley shrugged, all casual-like. "Fine."

"And if I don't get one past you?"

Christian could see Riley contemplating his answer, and even through the cage of Riley's goalie mask Christian could tell Riley's eyes were on him, assessing. They swept Christian up and down. Christian could almost feel the heat in his gaze as if Riley had reached out and touched him. He obviously had been wrong a few days ago...Riley *was* just as affected by him as he was by Riley. The heat shimmering between them, even from ten feet apart.... Like he could reach out and grab it, stuff it in his pocket. He was sure Riley was going to bet him a blowjob or something and his cock started to stiffen in his jeans.

"I want to know the reason you haven't moved back here," Riley said.

Instant boner-killer. No way was he telling Riley shit. Meant he'd have to work his ass off to get the puck past him. Riley hadn't played pro in two years. He was probably out of practice, right?

Wrong. The fucker stopped all twenty-six shots—yes, Christian counted—with seeming ease.

A kid, maybe five or six years old, wandered over from the house across the street to watch them play, so Christian kept his frustration to himself.

"What the f—heck?" He shot the puck one last time. It ricocheted off a post and embedded itself into a snowbank. Riley cackled like asshole he was.

So much for keeping his frustration to himself.

The kid—who looked like he was going to fall over and roll into the street he was wearing so many layers—took a step onto the ice, slipping and sliding in his snow boots. "Can I shoot, too?"

"Sure, kid." Christian handed over his hockey stick and, after a little bit of instruction, let him shoot the puck at Riley willy-nilly. The stick was much too big for him so his shots went wide most of the time, but when they didn't Riley— because he was Riley—let some of them in.

"I don't think I'm very good," the kid said after another shot went right instead of straight.

"Is it your first time playing?" Riley asked.

The kid nodded.

"Well, there you go. You just need practice. Want to switch places with me? Try and stop some goals?"

Christian watched the kid slide over to Riley. Riley removed his goalie pads so he could crouch to the kid's level and impart some goalie wisdom. Christian wondered for probably the hundredth time since Riley got hurt why the man hadn't gone into coaching. He was so likeable and he loved people. It just seemed like a natural fit.

Christian joined Trevor on the side of the rink and wondered why this kid wasn't paired with an adult. Had he run away to come watch them play? Sure enough, across the street a man stood at the end of his driveway, shaking his head. Christian lifted a hand to acknowledge him.

The man waved back. "Sorry about my son."

"No worries," Christian called back. "We were done anyway."

It was always amazing watching a kid pick up a hockey stick for the first time.

He watched Riley shoot the gentlest of shots at the kid. Some breezed by him, but when he managed to stop the puck, he smiled like Riley hung the moon and sun.

Which was basically how Christian felt about Riley, too.

"How come you know so much about hockey?" the kid asked Riley.

"I've been playing since I was seven. I used to play in the NHL, for Toronto."

The kid's eyes went huge. "That's my team!"

Christian couldn't help but chuckle.

"Do you know Patrick Finnegan?"

Patrick Finnegan was the new right-winger on Toronto's first line, poached from Detroit.

"I do," Riley said.

"You do?" Christian asked. Riley looked at him like, *of course.*

"He's my favorite player!" The kid practically yelled it.

"Jeremy!" the kid's father said. "Dinner!"

"That's me!" The kid slid across the ice to give Christian his hockey stick back. "Bye Mr. Hockey Player!" And he was gone.

Riley turned and pointed his stick at Christian. "I won the bet. Pay up! Start talking, T."

"I can't," Christian said. Riley narrowed his eyes. "Seriously. I've got to get home for Christmas Eve dinner with my mom."

"Fine. But don't think I won't collect."

Christian started removing his gear. "I'll come by later to say hi to your parents."

"They're not here, dude," Riley said, picking up his goalie pads from where he'd dropped them in the snow. "They moved to Florida last winter with my grandparents."

Christian's mom had told him that but, "And they didn't come back for *Christmas*?"

"Nah, they're on a cruise with some friends." Riley took off his mask, blond hair sticking up in every direction. "They're coming for a visit in a few weeks so we'll celebrate Christmas then. Dude, stop scowling. I'm twenty-seven, not seven. I can handle a Christmas by myself."

Nobody should spend Christmas alone. Especially not Riley. "What are you doing tonight?"

Riley looked at him. "Making myself a grilled cheese and watching *Die Hard* on TV?"

"No." Christian ignored Riley's sputtering—it really was cute that he thought Christian was going to let him spend Christmas Eve all by himself. In French Canadian culture, Christmas Eve was just as important as Christmas Day. He picked up his gear, grabbed Riley's net, whistled for Trevor, and started the short walk home. "Let's go, Riles."

Riley was muttering to himself but Christian could hear his footsteps behind him.

"T, I need a shower. I probably smell like the inside of a gym locker."

Hmm, good point. Christian stopped, reversed course, and trudged along the quiet street in the opposite direction. Riley was still talking to himself. Or maybe to the dog. Something about stubborn oafs and intruding on Christmas and tall idiots not letting him get a word in.

He was surprised when, from behind him, Riley told him to stop in front of a small, white, clapboard house. Riley's parents' house was still a few houses down. "What are we doing here?"

"I moved in here after my parents sold their house," Riley explained, arms full of goalie gear, his mask hanging around his wrist by a string.

Christian's jaw dropped. "You moved into your grandparents' house? Are you crazy?"

"Don't even start that shit." Riley took the net out of Christian's hands. "Come on, Trevor."

Christian froze on the sidewalk as Riley used the keypad to open the garage door then walk into the garage. He set the net in a corner before going into the house, the dog following like a faithful servant, the traitor.

Standing alone on the tiny sidewalk, Christian shivered. The wind was a knife in his bones and now that he wasn't moving he could really feel it. The street was dead quiet, as if not another soul lived here. The sun had set twenty minutes ago and the sound of the lake's waves gently lapping the shore and the wind in the trees combined with colorful Christmas lights reflecting off the snow sort of made it seem like he was the only survivor in a Christmas horror movie.

The door Riley had shut behind Trevor opened again. "Are you coming in or not?"

"Hell no."

Christian couldn't see Riley roll his eyes, but it was in his voice when he said, "I promise it's not haunted."

"Oh, yes, it is." He had nightmares about this house.

"Ever think that maybe your Ouija board ghosts will like it here? And they'll want to stay and not bother you anymore?"

Huh. That made a weird kind of sense. Maybe if his ghosts found buddies they'd leave Christian alone. Huffing, he followed in Riley's footsteps. Up the driveway, through the garage. He hesitated only briefly before stepping over the threshold and into the house. Ignoring Riley's amused smirk, he dumped his gear on the laundry room floor next to Riley's goalie pads.

"I'll only be ten minutes, max," Riley said. And stripped. Right there. In front of Christian. Socks, jeans, sweater, undershirt. It all ended up on the floor. At Christian's feet. Leaving Riley standing in front of him in nothing but his boxer briefs. And before Christian could look his fill, admire that tight ass in all its glory, those muscular thighs, that washboard stomach, the defined chest, Riley winked at him and walked out of the room.

He *winked*. What the ever loving goddamn hell did that wink mean? *Ha ha, you can look, but you can't touch?* Or, *Hey, T, the shower's this way*.

Did Riley want Christian to join him in the shower? If so, why didn't he just say so, instead of leaving Christian here guessing? Because had that been a real invitation, Christian would've been naked in a hot minute.

Or maybe that wink was just a friendly *See you in a few minutes* kind of wink. And yeah, fine. He was fooling himself. Coupled with a mostly-naked Riley and a sexy grin, that wink definitely wasn't friendly. Well, it was. It was just friendly in an *I want to do you* way, not a *Hey there, friend* way.

Looking down at the erection tenting his jeans, Christian

sighed, miserable. He spent so long debating whether or not to join Riley that he eventually heard the shower turn off. Wait, when had it turned on?

What a waste of a perfectly good opportunity to get naked with Riley. *Idiot*.

Naked with a wet Riley. Golden skin glistening with water. Christian would mouth water droplets down Riley's chest, over his stomach, to what Christian knew was an impressive cock. Where he'd lick the water off it before taking it in his mouth and—

Something brushed against Christian's leg and he jumped, so deep in his fantasy that he'd forgotten he wasn't alone in the house. His first thought was *Ghost*! But it was just Trevor, nosing around the dirty laundry pile.

"Jesus, Trevor," Christian croaked, relieved he wasn't staring at a shadowy specter. Trevor ignored him and trotted out of the room, dog tags tinkling.

A few minutes later, Riley returned. He got one look at Christian, still standing exactly where he'd left him not ten minutes ago, and burst out laughing.

"What?" Christian asked, grateful his boner had mostly disappeared. But it was making a comeback. Riley's laughter tickled his balls, and the way he was dressed in dark jeans and a blue, collared sweater? One of those with the zipper that only went about a quarter of the way down? Riley had it unzipped, showing off his strong neck and the column of his throat where a tiny bit of wetness caught Christian's eye.

"Why didn't you come in?" Riley asked.

Come in the shower? So Riley had wanted him to join him?

"You weren't confined to this room, you know."

Oh. Come into the *house*. Not the shower. And wow, he didn't expect that fierce disappointment.

Christian eyed the doorway just beyond the laundry room. "I'm not going out there."

Riley bent to put on his boots. "So what? Ghosts don't haunt laundry rooms?"

"*People*—*alive* people—don't even want to be in them. Never mind ghosts." He ignored Riley's indulgent smile and kept talking. Mostly to distract himself from how good Riley smelled. "There's nothing in here. What would they do? Play a trick on the owners by turning on the washer? Flick the lights on and off? They'd be better off haunting the bedrooms. People spend way more time in—"

"T?" Riley interrupted, standing.

"Huh?"

"Shut up and kiss me."

He didn't need to be told twice.

It was the same, and yet it wasn't. Christian knew the feel of Riley's lips on his, the way Riley's tongue felt sweeping inside his mouth. How hard Riley's body was underneath his hands. How good it felt when Riley inserted a leg between Christian's, bringing their erections in alignment.

What was new was Riley as the aggressor. He walked Christian backward until Christian's back hit the wall next to the door. Palming Christian's butt with one hand, he used the other to lift one of Christian's legs and settle it around his waist.

An aggressive Riley was hot as fuck.

They weren't careful with each other. Hands grabbed, teeth bit, hair was pulled. Christian moaned at the taste of Riley. Minty, like he'd just brushed his teeth. His hands found their way underneath Riley's sweater to scratch at bare skin.

Trevor's bark from another room finally brought them down from the high the kiss provoked. Breathing hard, they parted, but only as far as they needed to so they could see each other's eyes. Riley's were heavy-lidded, and one of his hands clenched on Christian's waist. Twin spots of color blushed his cheeks.

"We should go," Riley rasped, his gravelly voice tickling all of Christian's senses.

"Yeah."

But instead, Christian leaned forward to take Riley's mouth again. And this. This was the stuff first kisses were made of. This was less hunger, more passion. They slowed things down for this kiss. Hands petted and caressed rather than tugged and scratched. The scritch of Riley's five o'clock shadow on Christian's face made Christian shiver.

They pulled away with obvious reluctance, neither wanting to give up the other's mouth.

"We really should go," Riley said, even as his arms pulled Christian closer.

"We should," Christian agreed, eyes on Riley's mouth, the lips red and wet.

Growling softly, Riley gave Christian one last, hard kiss before releasing him to put on his coat. Whistling for Trevor, Christian opened the door to let them all out. Jesus, he was sweating like he'd run a marathon and he didn't even realize it until the cold outside air hit his flushed face.

The walk to Christian's mom's was silent, though Christian did have to scoop the dog's poop once. He snuck glances at Riley every few feet. He didn't realize Riley was doing the same with him until they locked eyes and smiled stupidly at each other.

"Fuck," Christian said when they reached his house not five minutes later. "I forgot my gear at your house."

Riley shrugged. "It's okay. It's not like you won't be back, right?"

The question was loaded with challenge and a small dose of insecurity. For the first time in his life, Christian couldn't get an accurate read on Riley. The guy who'd disappeared six years ago was now the instigator? Damn, but they really needed to talk.

But first, dinner with his mom.

Christian winked at Riley—*ha! Take that!*—under the glare of the porch light and led the way inside, where Trevor ran off down the hallway.

"Riley, *mon amour*!" Christian's mom appeared from the kitchen. "*Comment ça va?*" Christian couldn't help but laugh. *Mon amour*. My love. Even his mom liked Riley better than him. Not that Christian could blame her. He himself liked Riley better than pretty much anyone in the world.

HIS MOM MADE SO MUCH FOOD IT WAS ALMOST LIKE SHE knew Riley would be coming for dinner. She probably did in that sixth-sense way moms everywhere possessed.

Christian knew the food was delicious but he barely tasted any of it, too consumed with thoughts of Riley to really pay attention to what he was putting in his mouth. Of course that led to thoughts of Riley's dick in his mouth, and with his mom blathering away next to him, that was so not a thought to have.

But his mom could hold a conversation with herself without even trying. And that meant Christian could let his mind wander while inserting the occasional "Uh-huh" into the one-sided conversation his mother was unwittingly having with herself. And that also meant he could watch Riley while pretending not to, even though he was about 99.9 percent certain Riley knew what he was up to. Especially given the way he stared into Christian's eyes with a wicked gleam in his own as he licked his fork clean.

Christian gulped.

And wanted to curse because Riley, the jerk, was clearly

having no trouble holding up his own end of the conversation, piping in every once in a while with a follow-up question or comment to one of his mom's never-ending stories.

While subsequently rubbing his foot up and down Christian's leg under the table.

Just kill him. He was done. Had his mom not been there, nothing would've prevented Christian from vaulting over the table and attacking Riley.

But his mom was there. It was the only thing keeping his butt firmly planted on this side of the table.

A small part of him wondered if starting something up with Riley again was such a good idea. The last time they'd hooked up Riley had left him. Gone as if what they'd shared the night after his dad's funeral had been nothing worth remembering. For Christian, that night had been a rekindling of the passion between them. Fuck, he sounded like a Hallmark movie. But he'd thought that night had been...well, if not picking up where they'd left off over a year earlier then certainly starting something new.

Whereas to Riley, Christian had been a one-night stand. A trick. And the part of him that was still so deeply hurt by that wanted to run away and hide.

But he'd never run from his feelings. Especially not when it came to Riley. So the other part of him—a very large part—took caution, bundled it into a little ball, and threw it in the lake with the lost ships and nasty fish. Because what if he didn't take this chance? What if he just let Riley breeze through his life again like they'd never meant anything to each other? Would he spend the rest of his life wondering "what if"?

Yes. One thousand percent yes.

And if this went wrong and failed epically and his heart got shredded to bits again? Tough titties. At least he'd know that he'd tried.

Deciding two could play Riley's game, Christian hid a grin, slid one foot up Riley's leg until he reached his crotch and then pressed his toes against Riley's dick.

Riley choked.

"Riley! *Tiens. Bois de l'eau. Vite!*"

Christian couldn't help but laugh under his breath as his mom pounded Riley on the back and offered him a glass of water. Then she scolded Christian about how mean he was to laugh while his best friend might be dying.

Yeah. Dying of lust, maybe.

Since his mom had cooked he and Riley put the leftovers away and did the dishes. They even managed to sneak in a heated kiss while pressed up against the fridge when his mom went to set up the movie in the family room.

Once the dishes were done, they watched *A Christmas Carol*, the Mickey Mouse version. It'd been a tradition in his family for as long as Christian could remember. He and Riley sat as far apart from each other as they could manage without it looking like they were doing everything they could to avoid jumping each other's bones in front of his mom.

Trevor snoring in front of the fireplace added an interesting soundtrack to the whole situation.

After the movie was typically when Christian and his mom would exchange gifts. Christian hesitated. One: He didn't want Riley to feel left out. And two: He didn't want to give Riley his present in front of his mom. But Riley started making noises about heading home—Christian thought he did a very good job of masking his disappointment—but bless his mom. She wouldn't let Riley step foot out of the house until she'd given him her present.

Having Riley here reminded Christian of all the times they'd snuck into each other's windows on Christmas Eve as kids. At first it was because they wanted to swap presents at midnight. But after that first kiss in tenth grade it became about swapping something else at midnight. Mostly spit. And other bodily fluids as they grew older and bolder.

But also presents. Christian had a stack of Christmas and birthday presents for Riley at his apartment in Vancouver for every year they'd been apart since their break up. Because he was just humiliatingly pathetic enough that, even though they weren't together—hell, they hadn't even kept in touch—Christian had gone out to the store to purchase the perfect gift for Riley even though he might never see them. But that wasn't the point. The point was...

Well, Christian wasn't exactly sure what the point was. Other than to feel depressed and alone and to question all of his life choices, as if he wasn't already aware he was a huge goddamn fucktard for breaking up with Riley in the first place.

Long-distance relationships were hard. He'd always laughed at people who said that because really? How hard could they be? When you loved someone, you made it work. But he got it now. He did. Being in BC without Riley was almost impossible. Until it wasn't. Until, as time went on, things got just a little bit easier every day even though he never ever stopped missing Riley.

Then they'd get together. Over Thanksgiving weekend. For a few days over Reading Week. During Christmas. Summer. And whenever they could scrape the cash together to meet up in between holidays. Then he'd go back to his life in BC and Riley would head back to Colorado. Missing Riley became as familiar as his own face, especially for those first couple of weeks of separation. It was like a hole in his heart that wouldn't close. Still wasn't closed.

Until, with time, it got easier.

And the cycle would start all over again like a never-ending *Scrooge* movie.

He'd been calling himself an idiot since the day he told Riley he couldn't do it anymore.

Everything he'd ever wanted was right here, within reach. Christian sat in an armchair perpendicular to the couch. Partly because it was comfortable. Mostly because it gave him a direct line of sight to Riley.

Christian was nervous, and he never got nervous about anything. He hadn't even been nervous the first time he'd kissed Riley. He'd just been sick of dancing around his feelings that he'd mentally thrown his hands up in defeat and gone for it. Best decision he ever made.

Now he had a chance to fix what went wrong between them. Get his best friend back—and maybe the love of his life. It was hard to tell whether or not Riley wanted the same thing. Riley was obviously ready and willing to jump back into bed. Christian could start with that and work his way backward.

His mom got up from the couch after the gift exchange. (Riley had even pulled out a small gift for his mom out of his coat pocket.) "*Bonne nuit, mes amours*," she said, kissing both Christian and Riley on the head. "I'm so happy you're in each other's lives again," she whispered in his ear in French because Christian had never had a conversation with his mom in English in his life. They said good night in return and she disappeared down the hallway to her room, reminding him to shut off the Christmas tree lights before he went to bed.

Just the two of them. Christian and Riley. Fuck his life. He had no idea what he was supposed to do right now. Say goodnight? Watch another movie? Play Go Fish? Invite Riley to his room?

Riley, as usual, was the first to break the heavy silence between them. "I should go." He stood and Christian took a moment to admire his strong body. "I've been up since six."

To be fair, he did look tired, but the heavy-lidded blue gaze only served to make him look even sexier.

Christian followed Riley to the front door and stood awkwardly while Riley put on his coat and boots.

"So, uh," Christian said for lack of anything better to say, "what are you doing tomorrow?"

Jesus, seriously? He sounded like a fifteen-year-old asking someone out for the first time. *So, uh, what are you doing tomorrow? Do you want to, uh, like, get together? See, like, a movie or something?*

"Nothing much. Chilling in my pyjamas all day?"

"My mom and I are doing brunch. Do you want to, uh..." *For the love of God, don't say 'like.'* "...Like, come eat with us?"

Holy hell. It was like he was a pod person. What the hell was going on right now? He was *shy*? With *Riley*? Who he'd basically ordered to come to dinner with him and his mom earlier?

Somebody save him.

Thankfully, Riley did. By putting his mouth on Christian's.

Oh yeah. Yeah, yeah. This was good. No thinking involved. Just pure instinct. The feel of Riley in his arms had him instantly hard and if his mother wasn't right down the hall, he'd be on his knees with Riley's dick in his mouth pronto. Riley tasted like the one small cup of coffee he'd had with dessert: strong yet sweet. Their tongues dueled, vying for space in the other's mouth. Christian groaned when Riley sucked on his bottom lip, all awkwardness forgotten. His stomach fluttered and his heart raced when Riley pulled back and rested his forehead against Christian's.

Pressed together from thighs to forehead, Christian couldn't stop touching Riley. His arms, his shoulders, his neck. Pressing his thumb against Riley's chin forced Riley's mouth open and Christian swooped in, grinding his hard dick against Riley's while they kissed like it was the first time.

Riley pulled back, then came back in to give Christian a very soft closed-mouthed kiss. "I'll see you tomorrow," he whispered.

"Yeah."

Riley looked like he wanted to say something else. But all he did was smile crookedly, showing an unexpected hint of nerves. Christian held his face in his hands, swiping his thumbs against Riley's cheeks. Riley's hands clenched on Christian's waist, holding him tighter. Neither of them wanting to let go.

"Tomorrow," Riley finally said. And kissed Christian's cheek before turning and heading home.

CHAPTER
Four

AT A QUARTER TO MIDNIGHT, CHRISTIAN WAS LYING ON HIS bed in his old room, dressed down in sweatpants and the new forest green hoodie his mom got him for Christmas, watching a Youtube video of James Corden's Broadway riff-off with Neil Patrick Harris. Because who didn't love Neil Patrick Harris?

Plus Neil Patrick Harris was also superhot. The heavy boner in Christian's pants that was a living, breathing *thing* since his goodnight kiss with Riley twenty minutes ago...was still a heavy boner in his pants. And he couldn't watch porn and beat one off in his *mom's* house. Ew. Yeah he'd done it as a teenager, but he'd lived alone for years now and the prospect of masturbating with his mom down the hall was just... Just no.

Although if he didn't soften soon, he might have to consider compromising on his principles. Or stop watching NPH videos. Listening to the guy sing with confidence was such a huge fucking turn on. Kind of like watching Riley in goal.

Christian had been a little too obsessed with getting the puck past Riley earlier today to really notice at the time how damn good Riley looked in net. Like he belonged there. Like he was comfortable with having a fast, hard, rubber disc shot at his head.

Watching Riley in net when he'd played for Toronto had been unreal. The technical skills and commitment he brought to every game. His utter focus, as if nothing else existed except the puck and making sure it didn't get past him. Talk about a turn on. Riley didn't know it, but Christian had attended every Toronto vs Vancouver game in Vancouver that Riley had goaltended for.

And then he'd quietly left the stadium after each game without even trying to see Riley. Because Riley had been gone the morning after they'd last hooked up. Clearly that meant Riley didn't want to see him, right?

But Riley had welcomed him back to town with open arms—and a thoroughly unexpected full-on *hug*. It was such a juxtaposition to how they'd left things last time that it had Christian rethinking everything.

Fact: After they'd hooked up six years ago, Riley had been gone come morning.

Fact: They hadn't spoken since then. Not until a few days ago when Christian walked into Warm Glow.

Not so much fact as assumption: Riley wanted nothing to do with him.

New assumption: Riley's disappearing act was less about Christian, and more about Riley. About something going on in Riley's head he couldn't—wouldn't?—articulate back then. Something that Christian had been too preoccupied to notice.

None of this helped Christian right now but it did make him feel better about the whole thing. It still left him wondering where that left them now though. Those were answers he wouldn't get until he talked to Riley, but Riley had always been good at not talking about the important stuff.

A tap at his bedroom window. Christian's stomach jumped and his mouth went dry. Riley. Continuing their Christmas Eve tradition. He was surprised and yet not. Heart pounding, he opened the window to a grinning Riley.

"Hey," Riley said, voice low in deference to Christian's mom sleeping down the hall.

Turning so his back was to Christian, Riley sat on the windowsill, took off his wet boots outside, slid into the bedroom, reached back outside for his boots, set them on the towel Christian had already placed next to the window inside —because a guy could hope—and stood to shed his winter coat.

How could Riley be the only person in the world ugly plaid flannel pants looked good on? So not fair.

"I've come to collect," Riley said. He looked a little less tired than he had earlier, as though the fresh air gave him his second wind.

"Collect what?"

"On my bet. You owe me an answer."

The answer to why Christian still lived in Vancouver and hadn't moved back home yet.

"Here." In an effort to distract Riley, Christian handed him a wrapped gift, a box roughly twelve by twelve. "Merry Christmas."

If it was possible, Riley's grin got bigger. He sat on the bed and tore into the wrapping, opened the box and...

The smile fell off his face. Christian's stomach dropped to his feet. He'd done something wrong, he just knew it. For hours he'd debated whether or not to give Riley this gift. Worried that it would make Riley feel bad—

"T," Riley said, barely above a whisper.

—When he just wanted Riley to know how awesome he'd been, how much ass he'd kicked, and that Christian was always thinking about him.

"I..." Riley's words fell away.

The scrapbook was Riley in paper form. Christian had started it... God, he couldn't even remember what the first entry was. Riley's first game in net, maybe?

Pictures, newspaper articles, web articles, blog posts... hell, even Facebook posts and ticket stubs from every game Christian had ever attended. The book chronicled Riley's journey as a hockey player from the first game he'd played goalie as a kid until the very last game, two years ago with Toronto, when a player from the opposing team had run into him, breaking his leg and damaging his knee. It had effectively ended his pro hockey career. Christian had even found a newspaper article about Warm Glow in a recent issue of the *Oakville Beaver* that his mom had kept for him, and a blog post on blogTO called "The best little places no one knows about." He'd added them in to the scrapbook just last night.

Riley flipped through the pages, fingers touching a picture here, an article there. "T, I can't...I can't accept this. This is yours."

"No. It was always meant to be yours."

Riley's chin wobbled. He wiped his eye on his shoulder in that way guys-trying-not-to-cry everywhere had of pretending they just had to scratch an itch. Next to their eye. It made Christian's stomach hurt because at one point, Christian had been the one person Riley had let himself cry in front of.

Stretching out on the bed on his stomach, Riley propped the book up against Christian's pillows and continued flipping through it. Christian meant to give him some privacy, but he wanted to be near Riley, near his warmth, so he settled right next to him.

Riley grunted and flicked a finger against a group shot of the team they'd played for when they were sixteen. "I hated this guy."

"Me, too. Wonder if he still coaches."

"He does. In St. Catharines, I think."

"Poor kids. He's probably gotten more cynical with age."

Riley snorted. "No doubt. Man." He continued flipping through pages. "I haven't even seen half of this stuff." He stopped every once in a while to smile at something or reminisce about a moment or impart some gossip. So and so was married, or so and so retired from hockey, or remember this game? When we were still drunk from the night before and got reamed by the coaches?

"That was an awesome night," Riley said, stopping on a blog article from hockeyfights.com about the full line brawl that included the goalies during a Toronto vs Vancouver game.

"Yeah," Christian agreed. Even as he'd been hollering from the stands, his stomach had clenched with dread, afraid Riley might get hurt.

Riley was halfway through turning the page in the scrapbook when he noticed the ticket stub glued to the bottom right corner. "You were there?"

The surprised wonder in his voice and the pleasure in his eyes caused Christian's heart to flippity-flop in his chest. He tried to shrug as casually as he could. Like, *sure, I went to your games. No big deal. I'm just a pathetic SOB who wanted to feel close to you for a little while even though you didn't know I was there. I swear I'm not a stalker.*

Yeah. Awesome. He didn't mention that he'd been to every Toronto vs Vancouver game in Vancouver. Riley would figure that out on his own when he went through the rest of the scrapbook.

Riley didn't say anything but his eyes got dark and he swallowed roughly before glancing away. Christian could've sworn he saw Riley's hand tremble when he turned the page.

He slowed at a series of pages filled with articles about his injury and recovery. Christian almost hadn't included them, but they were a part of Riley's life, a part of who he was. It was important to remember the good and the bad. Riley didn't seem too bothered by them, and he stopped at a newspaper shot of himself coming out of the hospital surrounded by friends and family.

"How come you never..." Riley cut himself off and shook his head, flipping the page.

"How come I never what?" Christian asked, curious.

"You never...came to visit me. When I got hurt." Riley wouldn't look at him, and his voice was quiet and unsure.

Well, this was as good a time as ever to start that talk Christian wanted to have. No better time to put your feelings on the line than the present. "I did."

Riley's head whipped toward him so fast it made Christian jump. "What?"

"I came, but..." Christian shrugged again. "You had a lot of people here. Or there, at the hospital, I mean. Teammates, I guess? I dunno. And a bunch of family." Christian had recognized Riley's parents, grandparents, and even a couple of cousins from Quebec. "I didn't think you wanted me there."

"You flew all this way," Riley said slowly, incredulousness in his voice, "and what? Went right back?"

Another shrug. Because yeah, pretty much. Not even his own mom knew he'd been here for those few hours.

Riley huffed out a breath and it sounded broken and wet and—

"I'm sorry," he blurted. It sounded torn out of him with the rusty claw end of a hammer. "God, T. I'm so *sorry*." He rubbed his hands over his face.

"Riles—"

"No." Riley looked at him with eyes that were wet and a face drawn into tense, hard lines. "Is this why you won't come home? Because you think I don't...I don't want you here?"

Christian couldn't hold his gaze and when he heard Riley take a breath to speak, he mentally braced himself for whatever rejection was coming.

"I never meant for you to feel like that," Riley whispered. "Like you weren't important to me. You were. You *are*. You've always been the most important person in my life. Always."

"Then why did you leave? That night?" Christian didn't think he had to specify what night he was talking about. "I thought it was...We were going to..." He couldn't get the words together but Riley's nod said he knew what Christian meant. *I thought it was the beginning of us again.*

Riley blew out a breath. Closing the scrapbook, he moved it higher onto the pillow, then rolled onto his side. Christian mimicked his position so they both lay on their sides facing each other.

"I didn't come here to sleep with you that night, you know," Riley said. "I just wanted to make sure you were doing okay. I mean, I wanted to sleep with you. Obviously." Christian tried not to let that go to his head. Either one. "But at the same time, I didn't. I knew how hard it'd be after, going back to our separate lives, and... But then you started talking about quitting school and moving to Denver and I was so confused and I didn't want you to...to...to eventually regret making that decision and end up hating me," Riley finished, turning his face into the pillow. He said that last part so fast it made Christian's head spin.

"Riley, honey." The old endearment had Riley lifting his head to look at him. "Sometimes people make sacrifices for the people they love. And that was one I was willing to make so we could be together." It was getting hard to talk past the lump in his throat.

A tear escaped Riley's eye and dripped onto the pillow. "I'm sorry if I ever made you feel like hockey was more important than you. It wasn't. Never."

"Then why did you stay in Colorado that summer? For hockey?" All Christian had wanted was to spend a few weeks at home with Riley before Riley had to go back to Denver for hockey camp a couple of weeks before school started.

Riley gave him a self-deprecating smile. "I thought I could have it all. But sometimes you can't."

"Sometimes you can," Christian corrected. He ran his thumb over Riley's five o'clock shadow, the bristles gently scratching his skin, and placed a small kiss on the corner of Riley's mouth. "It just takes a while."

Riley squeezed his eyes shut; another tear leaked out anyway.

"I'm sorry, too," Christian said. Riley's eyelashes were wet when he opened his eyes to look at him. "For not being strong enough to hold on to you."

Christian was wholly unprepared for Riley to lunge at him. They lay on their sides, arms around each other, faces buried in the other's neck, legs tangled. Trying to control their emotions. Riley's shoulders shook under Christian's arms like he was quietly sobbing out all the pain and hurt and heartache of the last several years. Christian's own tears were surely drenching Riley's neck. But even as he cried for the lost years between them, wicked wings of glee unfurled in his heart. Riley didn't hate him! Riley said Christian was still important to him! Riley didn't leave that morning because he didn't want Christian; he left because he was scared. Riley was still his...um...

Okay, maybe they still had to talk about the future, but that could wait.

He tried to ignore the little tiny niggle of anger snaking its way into his brain. Because seriously, fuck them. Had they just *talked* all those years ago instead of assume shit, they would've saved themselves all this fucking drama. Jesus.

Whatever. Too late now. All they could do was move forward.

"Can we start over?" Christian asked. "Well, maybe not start over. There's probably too much history between us for that. But can we start...again? Or..." Fuck, he wasn't making any sense.

"Yes." Riley pulled away to look at him. His eyes were dry but his face was still splotchy. It made him no less beautiful. "Whatever you want, yes."

Whatever he wanted? Was Riley being purposefully vague? Or did he literally mean *whatever* Christian wanted. Because what Christian wanted was Riley. In his life. Forever. Maybe babies, but he wasn't a hundred percent sold on that. They could talk about that later, though.

"When you go back to BC, we'll still keep in touch, right? And you'll come visit more and I'll come visit you?"

When you go back to BC... A little piece of Christian died inside. All his hopes and dreams for their future, that brief moment when he thought they'd come true, curled up and shriveled in his chest. He forced himself to smile and nod before he started to cry again.

Riley was looking at him oddly, like he was trying to read his mind, so Christian forced his lips to curve higher. Riley finally smiled back at him and then looked behind him for... whatever it was, Christian didn't know.

"I need tissues," he said, and propped himself on an elbow to look over Christian's shoulder. "All the snot has moved into one nostril and I can't breathe from it." He plastered himself half on top of Christian trying to reach the tissue box on the night table.

Christian snorted and let the pain he wanted to wallow in creep to the background. He had Riley here, now. Better make the most of it while he could. He could go back to feeling pathetic and sorry for himself over the fact that Riley didn't want him forever when he got back to Vancouver.

When Riley finished blowing his nose, he stood to throw his used tissue away and grab something out of his coat pocket.

"Want your Christmas present now?" he asked.

Christian rolled onto his back and lifted his arms to stretch his back. "Is it magic chocolate?"

He waited for an answer and when none was forthcoming, looked at Riley, who stood on the side of the bed closest to the window, staring at the strip of skin visible between the bottom of Christian's hoodie and the top of his sweatpants. Biting back a smirk, Christian wiggled, forcing his pants down an extra smidge, just enough to reveal his hipbones and the top of the V that led to his dick. A dick that had finally softened during their talk but was now reawakening. Visibly so if the way Riley went cross-eyed was any indication.

"Wha...uh...huh?" Riley so charmingly articulated.

"Magic chocolate," Christian repeated, settling one arm behind his head and hooking the thumb of his other hand into the waistband of his pants. Testing the waters. *Whatever you want*, Riley said. Well, if Christian couldn't have Riley for forever, maybe he could have him for the next week and a half. Riley's mouth dropped open when Christian flexed his abs. Yeah. The man was down with that plan. "Did you get me some for Christmas?"

"What? No." Riley frowned and seemed to shake himself out of his stupor. "Here." He handed over a small box Christian hadn't noticed him holding. "Merry Christmas."

The box was about three inches by three and only about an inch thick, the size jewelry often came in. Christian sat up to take it. The red felt ribbon around the box was delicate to the touch. Ignoring Riley's fidgeting, he pulled gently so he didn't ruin it before tearing at the wrapping paper.

Riley took a seat on the bed next to him. Christian could see his thumbs jerking—a nervous tick he obviously hadn't gotten rid of.

"It's no memory scrapbook," Riley warned. "It's just a little thing..."

Inside the box was a hammered T looped onto a leather string.

"I had them make the necklace long enough so you could wear it under your shirt if you didn't want anybody to see," Riley was saying. "The metal is some type of special kind that's only found in BC. But the artist is a local one. He has a studio not far from here and he takes custom orders. Like this one."

Christian understood what Riley wasn't saying: This little T was a combination of both their worlds. A little piece of each of them.

His breath hitched and his vision got blurry but he would. Not. Cry. They'd already done that and he'd enough of overwhelming feelings for one night.

Instead, he smiled at Riley. "One of these days you're going to tell me what the T stands for."

"No."

Christian leaned forward, into Riley's personal space. "Yes," he whispered, his head rocking with the scent of Riley.

Riley's chuckle was soft. "No," he said, and closed the distance between them.

If Christian could spend the rest of his life doing nothing but kissing Riley, he'd be golden. Too bad nobody would pay for that and he needed to make a living somehow. Porn might pay. But nobody was seeing Riley's naked body but him, so porn was out of the question.

Pushing Riley onto his back, Christian followed him down, kissing his lips, his neck, his collarbone.

"I have ways of getting the information out of you."

Riley laughed. "They've never worked before."

Christian lifted the hem of Riley's hoodie. "I've learned new tricks since then."

A creak from down the hall. They both froze, Christian crouched over Riley with Riley's sweater bunched below his nipples, Riley with his legs spread, one leg thrown over Christian's calves.

Christian looked at Riley. "Ghost?" It was barely a whisper.

Riley raised an eyebrow. "Your mom?" he mouthed.

A door closed. The toilet flushed. The water ran in the sink. The floor creaked again.

Riley's smug smile said, *see? Told ya.*

Damn it! He couldn't give Riley a blowjob while his mom was awake.

"Christian, did you remember to turn off the Christmas tree lights?" she yelled in French from down the hall. Aaaand, sayonara erection. Nothing like a parent to cool your jets.

"I forgot," he said loud enough for his mom to hear him. "I'll do it now."

"Okay, goodnight. Goodnight, Riley."

"Oh, Jesus," Christian muttered, hanging his head. Underneath him, Riley started to laugh.

"See you both in the morning. I'm making crepes."

"Just kill me." He collapsed onto a giggling Riley and wished he could melt into the earth.

CHAPTER
Five

RILEY WOKE UP IN CHRISTIAN'S BED ON CHRISTMAS morning.

Alone.

For a brief moment, he thought Christian was getting his revenge by abandoning him after an awesome night. A sex-free night, but an awesome one just the same. But that idea didn't hold because, one: this was Christian's house. And two: Christian might be a grumpy motherfucker, but he wasn't an asshole. Not to Riley. Even when he'd broken up with Riley, Christian had been the nicest guy ever. Unstoppable tears dripping down his face, apologetic. Constantly reassuring Riley that this wasn't his fault, that it was *him*, Christian, who couldn't handle the separation.

Content to laze around in bed for a little while longer, he rolled onto his stomach and wished Christian was there so they could snuggle. The bedsheets smelled like him, a sort of woodsy scent Riley would forever associate with Christian.

Riley felt freer this morning. Their talk last night had cleared the air between them and he could finally breathe without it feeling like he was trying to do so with a noose tied around his neck.

But seriously, where was Christian? Why wasn't he snuggled up to Riley so they could rub one off on each other before they had to start their days?

"'Morning."

Riley raised his head. His eyes were blurry with sleep but he could make Christian out, sitting in a wingback chair next to the closet, feet on a matching ottoman, laptop on his thighs, wearing nothing but his boxer briefs and a scowl. Riley knuckled the sleep out of his eyes.

"Time's it?" he asked, admiring the way the dark hair on Christian's thighs and arms made them look so muscly. The size of those shoulders he could see over the laptop. His pouty mouth pursed in a frown. The disheveled dark hair that was, sadly, out of its pompadour style and hanging half in Christian's face and half straight up in the air. He looked like the character with the crazy hair from *Dragon Ball Z*. Riley's morning wood tried to convince him to make his way over there and straddle Christian's lap, but mostly he was happy to lay here and admire him. He went all mushy inside when he realized that, at some point, Christian had put on his T necklace.

"Seven thirty."

Oh, hell no. They'd spent hours talking after Christian's mom interrupted what would've been a stupendous blowjob, finally falling asleep around three in the morning. Seven thirty was way too early. Riley let his head drop onto the pillow and closed his eyes.

"Come back to bed," he said.

Christian grunted. "In a bit."

Riley's chest rumbled with annoyance. "What're you doing?" *Come cuddle with me!*

"Fixing your website."

"Huh?" Riley popped an eye open. "What? Why?"

"Because it's a piece of crap," came the honest reply. Maybe Riley ought to rethink the whole not-an-asshole thing.

"Hey! I paid good money for that."

Christian just looked at him.

"Fine," Riley grumbled. "I did it myself."

The tap-tap-tap of the keyboard filled the room. It should've been annoying, but he found it oddly soothing. Maybe because he knew it meant Christian was right *there*, within reach, and he could finally relax and stop dwelling on the past.

"How'd you get my login info, anyway?"

"Please. You've had the same username and password since high school."

And Christian remembered it. All these years later. Aw. Riley's heart swam with affection.

"You don't even have your menu on here," Christian muttered, click-clacking away. "Or pictures. Or information about who runs it or anything about the fact that you're nut-free and have gluten-free and vegan options. There's nothing about your delicious, magical hot chocolate. You should really advertise that. And you don't even say that you're a former NHL player."

Riley sighed. Seven thirty was way too early to talk business but fine. If Christian wanted to do this now, he was game.

"Because I don't want people coming into the shop because I'm a hockey player," he explained. "I want them to come because the food's good."

"No, you don't."

Groaning, Riley shifted until his head was half buried under his pillow. "You're making my head hurt."

"You want to advertise that a former NHL player owns, and works at, Warm Glow," Christian said, slowly, like he was explaining something to a toddler. Or a really old person. "Playing pro hockey makes you a celebrity in Canada, you know that right? So they come in to check out the shop and see what the hockey player is up to. And let's face it: probably also to get an autograph and a picture. But then they *come back* because the food is delicious and the ambiance is awesome and the service is flawless and you have magic chocolate."

Huh. That actually made sense. Everything except the magic chocolate, that was.

"How do you know this stuff?" Riley asked.

"I work in digital marketing." Christian said it like that was information Riley should've known. Which he did. He just forgot. Or maybe "forgot" was the wrong word. Purposefully didn't think about it? Yes, that was more accurate. He'd even thought once, very briefly, about asking Christian for help with the website. Back when he and Sam first started talking seriously about going into business together. But he'd chickened out and so had pushed the thought far away. Very, very far away.

"I also made you a Facebook page. And I bought you a domain name and signed you up for a new theme and re-skinned your WordPress website," Christian was saying now.

"I literally have no idea what you just said." How the hell was he supposed to make changes to his site if he didn't know how to *use* the damn thing?

Christian must've read his mind. "I'll write you a user guide."

Riley perked up. Though he didn't come out of his pillow nest. "Yeah?"

Knowing Christian, the user guide would have screen-shots and arrows and be so detailed even his Grandma Geneviève would be able to navigate the backend of his new website even though she'd never touched a computer in her life.

Speaking of backend...

"Can't you do that later?" Riley asked.

"Yeah."

Riley waited. When Christian didn't get the hint, he said, "So, why don't you?"

"'Cause I'm doing it now."

Oh, for the love of... The man was impossible.

"If I offer to blow you, will you come back to bed?"

Silence. Riley emerged from his nest. His hair was probably a mess and he had morning breath but they'd never cared about that kind of thing, so screw it.

Christian was looking at him curiously. "*Are* you offering to blow me? Or are you just saying that so I'll come cuddle?"

Riley thought about it for a second, then said, "Both. Blowjob first. Then cuddles." He lifted the bedcovers and patted the empty space next to him in invitation.

Christian took it, thank Christ. The man finally got the picture. Mornings weren't for *working*. They were for morning shenanigans.

The day's first kiss from Christian gave Riley butterflies. After last night it felt like they could do this without their past getting in the way. Christian's lips were soft against his, a direct contrast to how hard his body was. Christian clearly kept himself in shape, though he hadn't played hockey in years. Or maybe he did, in some kind of rec league in Vancouver. Something to ask about later. When Christian's tongue wasn't in his mouth.

Never taking his lips away from Christian's, Riley pushed Christian so he was flat on his back beneath him. Their legs tangled under the covers, thighs against thighs. Their erections collided and it felt fucking amazing even through cotton and they both groaned at the contact. Christian's hands slipped into Riley's underwear to cup his ass. Riley shivered and captured Christian's bottom lip in his mouth.

Riley was always surprised at how hot Christian's icy blue eyes could get. Like they were right now, charged with want and desire. Riley was sure Christian's passion was reflected in his own eyes.

Wanting Christian's dick in his mouth desperately, he kissed his way down Christian's chest, sucking a nipple into his mouth and—

"Christian! Riley!"

Riley froze. Christian's nipple popped out of his mouth.

"Are you fucking serious, right now?" Christian asked no one in particular.

"Crepes will be ready in ten minutes!"

"How does she *know*?" Christian asked, looking genuinely perplexed. "It's like she's purposely trying to cockblock me." Riley couldn't help it. He started to laugh. "My blue balls are gonna look like the fucking Smurfs."

Laughing too hard to hold himself up, Riley fell next to Christian on the bed. He noted that like Riley's, Christian's boner had all but wilted.

"Next sleepover's at my house," he said.

"Deal."

A FEW MINUTES LATER, RILEY LAY IN CHRISTIAN'S BED listening to the sounds of Christian rifling through his suitcase. God, he was tired. They'd fallen asleep so late and he'd been up at six yesterday morning and... Maybe he could take a nap later. Christmas Day was for doing nothing, especially when your family wasn't around.

Everything was so different now than it had been a few days ago. Sunnier. Not that his life hadn't been fulfilling. He had Warm Glow and Sam and his friends. But now he had Christian too and that just made everything better.

Not that Riley had any idea what the future held for them. By mutual agreement it appeared that that particular conversation was off the table for now and they were just going to...wing it? See where the next few days took them? It was probably not the greatest way to move forward. They'd end up hurting each other again that way. Riley told himself not to get his hopes up. They had the next eight days to get to know each other again and to—hopefully—fool around some. Then Christian would be on a flight to Vancouver and they'd go back to being just friends who visited each other every once in a while.

Could they really do that? Christian hadn't moved back home after he graduated from UBC because he thought Riley didn't want him here. Riley thought he'd made it clear last night that that wasn't the case. So maybe Christian would move back now.

Don't get your hopes up, you idiot!

His sigh was miserable to his own ears and he snuggled deeper into the bed, wishing he could go back to sleep. Only the thought of that potential afternoon nap convinced him to open his eyes.

Gaze snagging on Christian's scrapbook, Riley brought the bedcovers up over his mouth so he could smile stupidly without Christian seeing him. That scrapbook was proof that Christian hadn't forgotten about him, that he wasn't mad at him. Proof that Christian still cared. Christian hadn't mentioned it but Riley had seen the ticket stubs for his Toronto at Vancouver games. From what he could tell, Christian had been to all of them. He wanted to kick himself in the 'gnads for all those missed opportunities. What must it have been like for Christian to sit in the stands and watch him play? What must it have been like for him to come visit Riley in the hospital after his injury and see him surrounded by friends and family? Had he felt like an outsider looking in? Like he didn't belong? Like Riley had moved on with his life and didn't need him anymore?

Eyeing the scrapbook again, he swallowed past the ball in his throat. That scrapbook was proof that Christian was still taking care of him, all these years later and despite all those years apart and the way Riley had left things six years ago.

It had always surprised Riley that Christian didn't play goalie. He'd always been so protective of the people he loved, it just made sense. Sure, he was a grumpy fucker most of the time, but he took care of his family and he put everyone he loved before himself. And he took care of Riley. Always had. The way he was with Riley was a hard one-eighty to how he was with everyone else. More patient. More careful. More tender. Goalie just made sense, but no. The guy wanted to play defense.

Actually, now that Riley thought about it… Okay, yeah. Defense made a lot of sense. Defense was who Christian *was*. How had he not seen that before?

I'm sorry for not being strong enough to hold on to you.

Christian's words from last night reached down into Riley's soul and twisted it viciously. As Christian zipped his suitcase, Riley rubbed a hand over his chest. How did he convey to Christian that none of this was his fault? Or at least, not just his fault. They'd both fucked up.

Riley hadn't been lying when he'd told Christian that he'd thought he could have it all. It was why he'd stayed in Colorado for hockey camp that summer. He'd been a stupid kid, high on himself and his budding career, who thought the world was within reach and all he had to do was take it.

All he'd wanted, for as long as he could remember, was hockey and Christian. And for a while everything had been amazing and he'd had both.

And then he'd had hockey but no Christian.

Now he had Christian but no hockey.

It was blatantly obvious to him now in hindsight that he couldn't have everything, despite what Christian said. He wished someone would've told him that a long time ago. Because he would've picked Christian, hands down.

Rolling to the edge of the bed, Riley stuck an arm out from under the covers. "T?"

Christian finished pulling up a pair of faded-gray sweat-pants before crouching next to Riley's head. The way he took

Riley's hand and brought it up to his mouth to kiss the back made Riley's vision blurry.

"What's wrong?"

Please don't ever break up with me again.

If I asked you to move home, would you?

If I moved to Vancouver, would that be okay?

I'm sorry.

I was an idiot.

I missed you so much.

It was only the second time in his life that he had no idea what to say to Christian. How to express what he felt and what was in his heart. The first time was six years ago when Christian's dad died. What did you say to someone whose life had just shattered?

Nothing, as it turned out. Because there wasn't anything that could make it better.

The necklace around Christian's throat caught his attention. The leather cord was long enough that the T sat right between Christian's defined pecs. Riley reached out and picked it up, tracing his thumb over the metal.

The fact that Christian was wearing it meant everything. The fact that he wore it without knowing what it meant was even better.

Not that Riley would ever tell him that he'd started calling Christian T from the moment they met because he thought his name was Tristan for an entire week before he'd learned otherwise. *Christian* and *Tristan* sounded the same to his seven-year-old ears and he was still too embarrassed to own up to it.

Not to mention that telling Christian would ruin the magic of it at this point.

Forcing his melancholy mood away, Riley smiled at him and said, "Think the crepes are ready?"

Christian tilted his head and regarded him with those eyes

that saw too much. He seemed to debate with himself for a second on what to say. Finally, he smiled back and used the hand not in Riley's to pull the covers off the bed and thus off Riley.

"Let's go see."

They walked into the kitchen a few minutes later. Riley felt severely underdressed... It was *Christmas*. He should at least put on a pair of clean jeans and a nice shirt, not the flannel pants and hoodie he'd climbed through Christian's window in last night. But Christian was dressed similarly to him. And so was Sylvie Dufresne, as it turned out.

"Finally!" she said. "I was about to send Trevor to look for you."

Underneath the kitchen table, Trevor lifted his head at his name. When no one gave him any food, he settled his little black and white head back onto his paws.

Sylvie stood at the stove in a bathrobe over a nightgown, wielding a spatula like a goalie wields his hockey stick—with ease and experience.

Christian started pulling stuff from the fridge and pantry for the crepes—maple syrup, brown sugar, cottage cheese, fruit—so Riley made himself useful and set the electric teakettle to boil before getting plates to set the table. He and Christian moved around each other with ease, as though they'd done this a million times or like their awareness of each other caused them to instinctually sidestep each other.

Riley was grabbing cutlery from a drawer when Sylvie said, "So...how'd you sleep?" Was her voice full of innuendo or was that Riley's imagination?

Behind him, Riley heard Christian's forehead thump against the cabinet.

"Very well, thank you," Riley said, suppressing a chuckle.

"I don't know why you still bother sneaking in the

window," Sylvie said, flipping the crepe in the pan to cook the other side. "We have a front door."

"It's tradition," Riley explained.

"Ah. Yes. I understand. My son, he's big on tradition."

"He is."

"I'm standing right here," Christian reminded them unnecessarily.

"Yes, we're aware. It's impossible to miss your grumpiness taking up all this space in my kitchen."

Riley's snorted laugh contrasted sharply with Christian's almost-subvocal growl.

Christian scowled at Riley. "Don't encourage her."

Amused with them both, Riley finished setting the table. When the teakettle went off, he made a cup of tea with a touch of milk and honey and handed it to Christian before getting a mug of his own and pouring himself some of the coffee Sylvie had already made.

Turning for the bread box on the counter so he could make them some toast, he found Christian staring at his mug as if he'd never seen tea before.

"You're supposed to drink it," Riley explained.

Christian's stony look was unimpressed.

Chuckling to himself, Riley maneuvered around him to get the bread out of the bread box and—

—Jesus. Sylvie could start her own Warm Glow mini-market with the amount of stuff she had in here from his shop. Scones and tarts and four different kinds of bread and pound cake and croissants. What did she do with it all? It was way too much for one person. Shrugging, he took out every-thing but the bread and put it on the table. Whatever the reason, it was sweet that she wanted to support him. Five minutes later, bread toasted, fruit cut, and crepes made, they sat around the table and dug in.

Sylvie slathered a blueberry scone with butter. "These are my favorite."

Riley toasted her with his coffee mug before taking a sip. "I'll tell Sam you said so."

"How come you don't have donuts in your bakery?"

Blinking, Riley looked at Christian seated next to him, who looked equally as confused.

"Because Timmies," Christian said.

Sylvie waited for further explanation but when Christian went back to fixing his crepe she turned to Riley.

"Tim Horton's kind of owns the donut parade," Riley explained. He ignored how warm Christian's quiet chuckle made him feel and continued. "There's no sense in competing with them."

"I bet Sam makes better donuts," Sylvie said.

"She does. But still." Riley shrugged. "Timmies."

"These crepes taste like yours," Christian said to Riley before stuffing another bite in his mouth.

"Yeah," Riley said. "Because we use your mom's recipe."

Christian's eyebrows went up. "No shit? Mom, you're famous!"

A scramble came from underneath the table and then Trevor ran to where the open kitchen doorway and started barking at nothing.

"Trevor!"

Sylvie's yell stopped the barking, and the dog looked from the hallway to Sylvie and back. Finally, nails clicking on the kitchen tile, he trotted back to them and settled under the table again.

Christian peered down the hall as if the explanation for Trevor's weirdness would be written on the wall.

"They say dogs can see ghosts," Riley said.

The color drained from Christian's face and his eyes went so comically wide Riley could see the whites of his eyes. Swallowing his laughter, Riley reached out and squeezed Christian's thigh.

"Sorry," he said. "I'm wrong. It's not dogs. It's..."

"Cats!"

"Cats," he repeated, sending Sylvie a mental *thank you*. "It's cats. My mistake. Sorry, T."

Riley had to wonder if Christian would ever be able to sleep in this house without one eye open ever again.

TUCKED INTO A CORNER OF THE COUCH IN THE FAMILY room hours later, feet on the coffee table in front of him, Christian ignored the impromptu holiday party happening in his mom's living room and watched the *Supernatural* marathon on TV with the subtitles on. Riley was fast asleep, his back to Christian's chest, legs taking up the rest of the long couch. Christian had one arm wrapped around Riley's torso, his hand underneath Riley's hoodie to rest on his stomach.

It was three in the afternoon and Christian was honestly surprised Riley had stayed awake as long as he had. He'd looked tired as shit last night; this morning the bruises below his eyes were more pronounced. He'd fallen asleep on Christian almost an hour ago, sleeping through the doorbell, knocks, exclamations of surprise, shouts of "Merry Christmas!" and, now, the din of the crowd in the room across the hall.

At a population of two hundred thousand, the Town of Oakville—it should really be renamed the City of Oakville, but Christian could only imagine the huge pushback the town would get from...well, probably everyone who lived here—wasn't one of those towns where everybody knew everybody else. But in downtown Oakville and this small residential neighborhood south of Lakeshore all the way to the lake, between Navy Street to the west and Allan Street to the east, where families had lived for generations... It was like a mini village within a larger whole where everybody was up in each other's business all. The. Time.

He was glad his mom had all these people around her. With him living all the way across the country, he didn't want to think of his mom out here all alone. But she had a big group of friends and still worked part-time and was part of a whole bunch of clubs. They were what had made it okay for him to head back to Vancouver after his dad died.

Christian must've fallen asleep at some point because he suddenly became aware of a whispered conversation next to him.

"Are they back together?"

"Aren't they just the sweetest?"

"Well, I don't know about back together, but at least they're friends again," came his mom's accented English.

Christian would've sworn he heard the distinct *snap* of a phone camera.

"Do you think Riley knows how tightly he's holding on to Christian's arm, even in sleep?"

"I think they're both too dumb to know anything."

"Oh, Sylvie, dumb's a harsh word."

A huff of breath. "You're right." Silence for a second, then, "What's the opposite of perceptive?"

"Obtuse?"

"Yes! That's a good word. Obtuse, both of them."

Rubbing the sleep out of his eyes, Christian lifted his head off the back of the couch and looked at the four women huddled together on the other side of the coffee table. Not a guilty look among them for spying or gossiping without remorse.

"He thinks he's scary when he scowls like that," his mom whispered loudly to her friends.

All four of them giggled under their breath before shuffling out of the room.

Jesus. The humiliation he subjected himself to for his mom's amusement.

Trevor padded into the room, looking like he'd gotten into the keg at a doggie party. Hair standing straight up all over his small body, dog collar askew, he fell onto the rug in front of the fireplace with a tired sigh.

That's what you get for not being able to hold your liquor.

The thought made Christian snort. Fuck, he must be tired if he was imagining canine keggers.

He watched the last few minutes of the *Supernatural* episode playing on TV and was halfway through the next one when Riley finally stirred, thank God. Christian had been in the same position for over two hours. His left asscheek was numb, the arm around Riley was sore, he needed to stretch out his knees, and Riley's body heat was making him sweat.

"Is this the same episode?" Riley's voice was deeper, rumblier, with sleep. It reached right into Christian and made him shiver.

"No. There's a marathon on."

"A *Supernatural* marathon on Christmas?" Riley chuckled. "Sure, why not?"

Riley moved so that he was lying fully on his side on the couch, head on Christian's thighs. It was enough that it let Christian shift position so that he wasn't uncomfortable anymore and he could remove his hoodie, leaving him in a simple T-shirt, without disturbing Riley.

"Why do you watch this if you're afraid of ghosts?"

"I'm not *afraid* of them." Christian scoffed and ran a hand through Riley's dark blond hair. "I just don't like them."

"Uh-huh." Riley's voice sounded drowsy. "You won't even come into my grandparents' house. And you've taken the

Oakville Historical Society's ghost tour. You know all the Oakville ghosts are friendly."

"Lies."

Riley's laughter rumbled against his thighs.

"I can switch this if you want," Christian offered, nodding at the TV. "We can watch a movie."

"No, this is good. I missed a few episodes last season. I think this might be one of them."

"You still watch this?"

"Of course. Sam and Dean."

That was really all the explanation needed, though Christian wanted to think that Riley had kept up with the show because it used to be their thing. They used to watch it together every week growing up. Even in university they'd watch while Skyping each other. The fact that Riley had kept watching over the past few years made Christian smile. He wrapped an arm around Riley's torso, resting his hand on Riley's stomach. In a move that made Christian's heart melt, Riley twined their fingers together.

"I guess Warm Glow is closed today?" Christian asked.

"Yeah. Tomorrow, too."

"Tomorrow? But it's a huge revenue day with the Boxing Day sales. You'd get a lot of foot traffic." The look on Riley's face a few days ago when Christian had asked him if the bakery was having financial difficulties had set off alarm bells in his head. It was why he'd started working on Warm Glow's website this morning. Why he'd put feelers out for advertisements to local newspapers. Why he'd reached out to some of the Greater Toronto Area's big-name bloggers and created a Facebook page.

"Yeah," Riley said, "but most of the stores on Lakeshore will be closed so Sam and I didn't see a point in opening."

"Is the store doing well?" Christian was *dying* to know. "It seems like it is based on the amount of people I saw in there when I came by."

Riley didn't say anything for a minute, and just when Christian convinced himself he wasn't going to answer, Riley sat up and tucked his right leg under himself on the couch so that he faced Christian. His eyes looked clearer and more alert, the lack-of-sleep gone from his face. The scruff on his jaw and cheeks was sexy as hell and Christian didn't bother resisting the urge to reach out and run a palm over it.

"I don't know if I should be worried," Riley said, tilting his head so Christian had better access. "The shop's not doing bad. In fact, it's doing really well even though we've only been open two and a half months. But it's not paying for itself yet, which... I don't know. Everything I've read and heard says that that's normal, that it takes a while."

"It does." Christian removed his hand from Riley's face and placed it on Riley's knee.

"I have money saved up." Riley's smile was rueful and he glanced away to play with Christian's fingers. "I played for the NHL for three years, so it's not like I'm counting my pennies. And sometimes I think I should just use my savings to cover any deficits with the shop. And I have been doing that, but I can't do that for the long haul. That's not a very good business model."

"You need to do more marketing. Better marketing."

Riley rolled his eyes. "Yes, you weren't exactly subtle this morning when you were knocking my website."

"The new one will help," Christian promised. Riley didn't look convinced but Christian knew what he was doing.

They spent the rest of the afternoon tangled together on the couch watching a sometimes-scary, sometimes-corny, always-awesome sci-fi show with a pair of hot actors. They only moved to reposition themselves, get food, or go pee. Eventually his mom's friends left and Sylvie joined them in the family room. They switched from *Supernatural* to *The Descendants* because his mom had an obsession with Golden Globe winners.

It was relaxing and pressure-free and the best Christmas since Christian's dad died.

CHAPTER
Six

THE SLEEPOVER AT RILEY'S DIDN'T HAPPEN UNTIL A COUPLE days later. They spent Christmas night at Christian's mom's because Christian didn't want to leave her alone on Christmas. So they behaved themselves in Christian's bed and kept things mostly PG-rated.

Boxing Day saw them at Glen Eden in Milton for some snowboarding. A fact that Riley was sorely regretting the next day on his walk home from Warm Glow after the day from hell. He knew he should've skied instead, but it just wasn't as much fun as snowboarding even if snowboarding made his injured knee ache from being kept in the same position for hours. Added to today's full day on his feet serving customers and his knee felt about the size of a basketball and as sore as a hockey puck to the teeth.

He needed an ice pack. An anti-inflammatory. A painkiller. Someone to kiss it better.

Someone named Christian.

Gritting his teeth, Riley made it to the stop sign before he had to stop and breathe through the pain. He'd overexerted himself the past couple of days, he knew it. His knee hadn't hurt this bad since physical therapy.

He almost texted Christian to cancel their plans for tonight because the thought of standing in his kitchen to make dinner made him want to whimper pathetically. But Christian would see right through him, would know that Riley was cancelling because he hurt—he'd seen the winces Riley hadn't been able to conceal on the drive home from the slopes last night—and would immediately blame himself for ever having suggested they go snowboarding in the first place.

Or, Riley could call Christian now, tell him to borrow his

mom's car and come pick Riley up at the corner of Lakeshore and Thomas. Then he could let Christian take him home where Christian could fuss to his heart's content. Which would help assuage any guilt Christian would unquestionably feel for something he perceived as his fault.

Option two, please.

At least it wasn't too cold out while Riley waited for Christian to come get him. In fact, it had warmed up considerably over the past couple of days, the temperature hanging somewhere just below zero. It was snowing big, fat, lazy flakes that settled over old, dirty snow, giving downtown Oakville a postcard-perfect feel, especially with the Christmas lights glowing in storefront windows and the old-fashioned streetlamps decorated with wreaths and tiny white lights.

Snowflakes landed in his hair and he blinked some out of his eyes. Cars passed him on the street, none of them Christian. That was okay though because he didn't mind the cold, never had, not like Christian, and he was happy to let the cool air numb the pain in his knee slightly.

A car pulled up to the curb minutes later, four-way blinkers flashing. Before Riley could take a single step toward it, Christian was already out the door and two-timing it toward him.

"I can walk," Riley grumbled.

"Shut up and lean on me," Christian said. With an arm around Riley's waist, Riley was able to lean on Christian as he hobbled to the car, saving him from putting his entire weight on his right knee. He settled into the passenger seat of Christian's mom's SUV and watched dumbfounded while Christian went so far as to lean in and buckle Riley's seatbelt.

"I'm not an invalid," Riley joked.

"Shut up," Christian said again.

In the yellow glow of the overhead light, Riley could

clearly see the lines of strain bracketing Christian's eyes. His lips were so tightly pressed together they were edged in white. Before Riley could address Christian's whole public-enemy-number-one schtick and kiss away his self-recriminating frown, the door closed and Christian was rounding the hood to get in on the driver's side.

Pulling away from the curb, Christian said, "We'll be there in just a minute," with a tight voice as if Riley didn't know it only took about thirty seconds to drive home from here.

Determined to replace Christian's furrowed brow with a smile, Riley said, "Shut up and let me groan in pain." And proceeded to groan so theatrically it sounded like he was either being rather epically murdered in a Greek tragedy or having the orgasm of his life.

It made Christian laugh. Mission accomplished.

He shoots, he scores!

Threading his fingers with Christian's over the gearshift, Riley smiled at him. "Thanks for coming to get me."

Christian's answering smile was strained, but at least it was there. Riley was glad he hadn't sucked it up and tried to walk home. Firstly, he didn't think he would've made it without succumbing to tears of pain. Secondly, it was worth it, making himself vulnerable to make Christian feel like he was helping to fix something that he blamed himself for.

Once parked in Riley's driveway, Christian made him wait in the car until he could come around and help him out, then up the walkway and up the one stair onto the porch and into the house. Christian seemed to forget all about his fear of ghosts as they took off coats and boots in the front hallway. Then he helped Riley into the kitchen, sat him at the kitchen table, took an ice pack out of the freezer, wrapped it in a dish towel, and handed it to Riley along with a glass of water and the bottle of pain meds sitting on the countertop.

Yes, *feared* ghosts. Please. Riley could smell a lie on Christian a million miles away and *I'm not afraid of ghosts, I just don't like them* was one of them. Christian was afraid of ghosts like other people were afraid of heights. It was irrational—there was no such thing as ghosts—and Riley had no idea how this fear had started or why—wasn't even sure Christian knew—but there it was. And Riley's house—formerly his grandparents' house—was so not haunted, thank you very much. It was an old house: it creaked, it moaned, it was drafty. Riley had grown up a few houses down and he'd spent a lot of time here growing up and had seen nary a single ghost.

Because they didn't exist. But try telling Christian that.

He watched Christian take off his watch, wash and dry his hands, then remove the cream, cheese, garlic, and chicken breasts from the fridge.

"I was going to make fettuccine alfredo with chicken," Riley said from his perch on a kitchen chair, ice pack on his knee.

Christian's answering expression said, *duh. What else?* As if he hadn't figured it out based on said ingredients sitting in the middle of the fridge when he opened it up.

Riley just grinned at him.

Watching Christian cook was awesome. Riley knew he had a goofy grin on his face, but the meds were making him kind of high and he didn't care. Wearing jeans and a zip-up sweater, Christian worked the kitchen like he was a Master Chef. Riley watched him grate cheese, mince garlic, and measure out cream until the pain in his knee started to recede. When the ice pack soaked through his jeans, he got uncomfortable and stood to—

"Where you going?" Christian zeroed in on him like a coach assessing his players' skills.

"To change?" Riley said, feeling a little off-kilter at having all of that sudden Christian-attention on him. His eyes raked Riley up and down like he could see everything that hurt.

"I'll help you." Christian moved the pan off the burner and put the chicken breast package back in the fridge.

"I can make it down the damn hallway." Riley knew Christian was going to fuss, but his bedroom was only fifteen feet away.

"Shut up."

Man, Riley was going to have to teach him some new words.

Christian hovered, sharp eyes on Riley while he changed into a pair of sweats and an old T-shirt, never ogling for more than a few seconds, making no attempt to get frisky. It showed how much Christian blamed himself for Riley's current predicament.

"You know," Riley said, fed up with Christian's pity party, "I didn't have to go."

"Go...change?"

Riley snorted a laugh despite himself. "Go snowboarding. This is my own damn fault. I didn't have to say yes when you asked."

"I shouldn't've asked," Christian said, wincing. "I forget sometimes that you can't do some stuff like you used to. You're just so...*whole*. So healthy. I forget."

That was possibly the nicest compliment anyone had ever paid him. He didn't want people to remember him as the goalie who had to retire due to injury. He'd worked really fucking hard to keep in top shape, both mentally and physically.

Shoving the pain in his knee to the background, Riley took the three steps needed to close the distance between himself and Christian. Eyes snagging Christian's, Riley walked him backward until his back hit the bedroom wall, and then he attacked Christian's mouth like they hadn't seen each other in years instead of less than twenty-four hours.

When Christian gasped, Riley invaded his mouth with his

tongue, sweeping across his teeth and sucking in Christian's taste. Christian's arm came around him, bringing them so close not even air fit between them. Riley pulled back, breathing hard. Something about the drugged look in Christian's eyes tamed Riley's urgency a bit. Leaning in for another kiss, he kept this one slow though no less passionate.

He ached to make Christian his again. Christian was heading back to BC in a few days—something Riley knew but tried not to think about. Starting something sexual probably wasn't a good idea. They'd both get hurt when Christian left. But if Christian was on board with this—and he definitely was based on the way he kissed back, based on the way he walked Riley backward so that he tumbled onto the bed— then Riley was jumping in with both feet and not looking back.

No regrets.

Riley hoisted himself up the bed so that he was fully on it, Christian crawling up his body to meet him. Christian's eyes were warmed blue opal. His lips met Riley's again and he settled all his weight on him, careful of Riley's knee. It pushed Riley deeper into the mattress and he moaned at the exquisite feel of their bodies finally, *finally* coming together.

This. This was his kiss to make it better.

The kiss went from languid to heated in no time and clothes came off faster than Riley could say "Fuck me."

It was Christian, as it turned out, who pulled his mouth off Riley's nipple to say, "Fuck me." Riley moaned at the words, the heat of them making his balls tingle.

Christian might want Riley to fuck him but he didn't stop making his way down Riley's body long enough for Riley to pause and think. Just worked his way down, down, licking over pecs and abs and hipbones until he swallowed Riley's painfully erect dick without so much as a *Hang on to something, I'm going in.*

"Fuck, T," Riley sobbed, fisting a hand in Christian's hair and holding on for dear life. Christian's mouth was hot and wet and Riley dug his toes into the bedcovers and tried not to come too soon. Christian's mouth might make him see stars, but being inside him? The thought made him moan so loud, Christian actually stopped what he was doing to ask if he was okay.

Riley had to laugh. "No. No, I'm not okay." God, Christian's mouth, all wet and pouty from being wrapped around Riley's cock, was going to kill him.

"Your knee?" Christian looked like he was about to put a stop to everything to go search for a new ice pack.

Fuck his knee. If it still hurt, Riley couldn't feel it.

"No. My dick. It needs to be inside you."

Christian rolled his eyes. "And you say my jokes are lame."

"That wasn't a joke," Riley protested. In fact, he was so dead serious that he rolled slightly to reach into the night table for the lube. "I don't joke about dicks."

"*Every* guy jokes about dicks."

"Good point." Riley conceded that one. "But I don't joke about them in this kind of situation. When it comes to sex, dicks are a serious matter."

"Jesus, Riles. Stop talking and put yours in me already."

Aw, his guy was such a romantic.

So romantic that he growled in impatience and snatched the tube out of Riley's hands. Christian sat up on Riley's thighs and Riley watched him pour a dollop right onto Riley's dick and stroke. The sight, the *feel*, of Christian's hand touching him was too much. It was electricity zapping his skin. The sight of Christian's own erect dick, bobbing straight out in front of him, his ropy forearms, defined abs and arms...the way those eyes looked at Riley as if he couldn't wait for Riley to come all over him... It took Riley's breath away.

But none of that even came close to how hot it was watching Christian dribble some lube onto his fingers and then use those fingers to reach back and stretch himself. He kept his eyes on Riley's the whole time and Riley held his gaze as Christian's eyes went from blue opal to stormy sky. His mouth dropped open, body going taut. Riley did what he'd wanted to do since Christmas Eve and reached out and took Christian's dick in his hand, jacking him while Christian stretched his hole.

"Enough," Christian growled and, lifting himself up, positioned Riley's dick at his entrance and sank down ever-so-slowly. Slow enough to get used to the stretch. Slow enough for Riley's heart to double-time it against his ribs. Slow enough for a flush to overtake Christian's chest. Riley saw it move upward over his neck and into his cheeks. The look on his face was pure bliss.

Once he was fully seated inside Christian, Riley could feel their ballsacks brush against each other, could feel the dark hair on Christian's inner thighs brush his own legs.

Christian leaned forward, over Riley's torso. Their eyes connected from millimeters away. Riley buried his hands in Christian's hair, messing up his carefully styled 'do. Christian's arms snaked around Riley and slid down to his ass, where he grabbed hold, pushing Riley even further into him. Fuck, that was so good, Riley swore the damn stars multiplied by the thousands.

"Hi," Christian whispered, lips brushing Riley's.

"Hi." The emotion he saw in Christian's eyes had Riley rethinking everything he thought he'd ever known about love and passion and desire. Rethinking his past. Rethinking his future. He knew Christian was his future. A life without Christian would be gray and hazy.

The moment stretched. And though they were both turned on and ready to move, it seemed they were both also content to hold each other, to rediscover what they once had, to let the knowledge of what they could have again settle in and grow roots.

Christian bore down on him and Riley swore his eyes crossed. Christian grinned knowingly and started rocking. Their mouths met and clung. Riley started to move. Slowly at first, and then faster.

"Right there," Christian whispered, ripping his mouth away. "That's the spot." He buried his face in Riley's neck.

Licks of fire winged up Riley's spine and he pumped, pumped, pumped into Christian and it felt so agonizingly delicious, he was afraid he'd come too fast.

"T..."

"Close. So close." Christian lifted himself up on his fore-arms, giving Riley space to reach between them and grab his cock. He shot like a hockey puck going a hundred and fifty kilometers an hour, spewing come all over Riley's stomach.

The way Christian's thighs squeezed his own, the way he bit Riley's shoulder when he came, the feel of Christian in his hand... Riley's balls drew up and he threw his head back and came with a strangled shout.

Collapsed together, legs tangled, breathing hard, Riley smiled at the ceiling. Sex had only ever been this awesome with Christian. Years later and it was still just as potent.

"Jesus fuck," Christian whispered raggedly into his neck. "I need food before we do that again."

Riley's laugh pushed him deeper into Christian. He must've hit the sweet spot because Christian stiffened and hissed out a breath.

"Sorry," Riley said, knowing how sensitive Christian got after coming. He pulled out of Christian and watched Christian's body ripple as he shifted to lie on the bed. Riley made a move to get up, but Christian stopped him with a hand on his arm and a quick kiss to his cheek.

"I'll go." He disappeared into the en suite, Riley's come dripping onto the back of his thigh. It shouldn't have been as hot as it was, but damn. That sight never got old. They'd never once used condoms although they probably should've at least had the discussion tonight given how long it'd been. But when you trusted someone as much as Riley trusted Christian, the point was moot anyway. Christian would've brought up the need for them had he had to, same as Riley would've.

Christian returned from the bathroom, where he presumably cleaned himself. He used a warm washcloth to clean Riley's stomach and cock, then wrapped an ice pack he pulled from seemingly nowhere with Riley's abandoned T-shirt, setting it on his knee.

Riley went to protest, but okay, yeah. Now that he wasn't consumed by Christian and lust and Christian, his knee fucking hurt.

"Do you need an anti-inflammatory?"

Fussy Christian was back, but Riley didn't mind. Riley'd fucked the scowliness out of him, so now Christian's concern was a warm blanket instead of a prickly thorn in his side.

"Let's see if the ice pack works first."

Christian stood by the bedside, arranging and rearranging the T-shirt-wrapped ice pack on Riley's knee. Finally satisfied with his handiwork, his gaze moved upward, over Riley's softened dick, his six-pack, his arms, up his chest. Riley preened when Christian swallowed roughly.

"Like what you see?"

Immediate scowl. "You don't need me to tell you you're gorgeous."

It went to Riley's head anyway. How could it not?

"Come here," Riley said, spreading his legs, careful not to dislodge the ice pack.

Christian raised an eyebrow at him, but he came. Settling

between Riley's legs, torso half on Riley and half on the bed, he propped his head in one hand and traced Riley's smile with the other. The gesture made Riley's stomach flutter with affection.

"I should go make dinner," Christian said, not moving.

"In a minute."

Christian laid his head on Riley's shoulder and flung an arm around his waist. His sigh brushed Riley's neck and had Riley breaking out in goosebumps. It was nice, just lying like this, no expectations. The silences between them had never been awkward or weird, and the same held true now. It was soothing. Calming.

Riley ran a hand along Christian's arm, over the ropy forearm and muscled triceps, and back down again. His form reminded Riley of a question he'd wanted to ask him a few days ago but had forgotten about.

"Do you still play hockey?"

"Yeah." Christian's answer rumbled against his throat. "In a rec league in Vancouver."

"Is it the same league you joined when you first moved out there after high school?"

"One and the same. We get some new players every year, and we lose others. But there's a group of us that's been there for a while."

"Sounds awesome." The wistful quality of Riley's voice caught him by surprise.

"Do you miss it? Hockey?" Christian's question was tentative, like he thought it might be a sore topic. But Riley had never shied away from talking about hockey or his injury or his forced retirement. It had been his life for so long, there was no point in pretending it hadn't happened.

"All the time."

Christian didn't seem to know what to say to that. He stayed quiet, which Riley appreciated. Empty platitudes were useless and advice was simply unwanted. Christian knew him well enough to know that.

Riley traced figures lightly on Christian's arm. It must've tickled because Christian jerked and snorted. Chuckling, Riley—

Wait a second.

The shift of Christian's arm across Riley's stomach revealed a small tattoo on the inside of Christian's wrist, right where his watch usually rested. Riley lifted Christian's arm and brought it closer so he could see it better, ignoring how Christian tried to pull away.

Riley's throat closed. His eyes burned. "You actually did it." He forced the whisper past the lump in his throat.

"'Course I did." Christian's voice was equally as quiet.

Everything, literally everything Christian had done since he'd walked back into Riley's life last week had served to prove to Riley that, despite how he'd left things six years ago, Christian hadn't forgotten him. And he was still taking care of him. Christian helped out at Warm Glow, he fussed over Riley's knee, he gifted him with an amazing memory scrapbook, he made sure his Christmas wasn't spent alone with his TV. Now this. This tiny tattoo shouldn't have meant so much, not all these years later. But it all proved that Riley's heart and soul still belonged to Christian and always would.

97. Riley's jersey number.

Remarkably, it was tattooed on the inside of Christian's wrist.

It was also the year he and Christian met on the first day of second grade. Had Christian ever made that connection? They'd both been transplants from Quebec, neither knowing a lick of English. Their last names—Deschamps and Dufresne—meant that, alphabetically, they sat next to each other in school. Instant friendship. And the fact they lived in the same neighborhood? Even better.

"One day," Christian had said sometime in high school, when it became clear that Riley was developing into a wickedly talented goalie, "you're going to be drafted into the NHL. And when you do, I'm going to get your jersey number tattooed somewhere."

Riley had snorted. "No, you're not."

"Am, too."

"Yeah, right. Where?"

"Dunno." Christian had shrugged. "Somewhere important."

His wrist. The inside of his wrist. A place not easily hidden from others. A place where he'd likely see his own tattoo every day for the rest of his life. A reminder of the promise he'd made. A reminder of what they'd once meant to each other, what they'd lost. The friendship they'd left behind. Behind, but never forgotten and always treasured.

The ice pack slid off his knee when he shifted to his side so he could face Christian. He didn't bother blinking the wetness out of his eyes. Christian deserved to know how important, how loved, how cherished the tattoo made him feel. He pressed a closed-mouth kiss very gently to Christian's lips.

"Thank you," he said, heart too full for more.

Christian only smiled softly and used the arm around Riley's waist to pull him closer. Riley tucked his head underneath Christian's chin and let himself drift.

It felt like only minutes later when his stomach growled. Chuckling, Christian pressed a kiss to his forehead and disentangled himself.

"I'm going to make dinner before our stomachs start an even louder campaign."

"I'll be right out," Riley said, unashamedly watching as Christian pulled his jeans and T-shirt back on and left the room.

Riley set the melted ice pack in the bathroom sink and dressed in a pair of sweats and a hoodie. Still a little emotionally raw from that 97 on Christian's wrist, he took a second to splash cold water on his face. A gesture like Christian's deserved reciprocation and Riley had just the thing. The reading lamp on the night table on the far side of the bed was where he hung the—

Riley looked. Looked again. Scoured the top of the night table with his eyes. Searched under the bed and on the floor by the window. His heart beat too fast and he wasn't breathing properly. Where the fuck was it?

Okay. Everything was okay.

Retrace your steps.

The last time he'd worn it was...before Christmas. No. Christmas Eve. He'd been at work, then played some pond hockey with Christian. Then they'd come back here so he could shower. Hot make-out session in the laundry room, then the walk to Christian's. Dinner with Christian and Sylvie, *A Christmas Carol*, gift exchange. Second hot make-out session at the front door. He'd walked back home to change and get Christian's Christmas gift...

And had taken it off on his way back to Christian's for their traditional sneak-in-the-window-and-exchange-presents night. Knowing they might lose some clothing that night, not wanting Christian to see it, he'd taken it off and...

He practically ran down the hall to the front entrance, stupid bum knee hindering his speed. His eyes watered again and his nose burned. Ignoring the shaking in his hands and the constriction in his chest, he searched first one coat pocket, then the other.

And wanted to sob in defeat.

It wasn't there. The necklace he'd had made to match the one he'd gifted Christian, it was just...gone. Had it fallen out at Christian's? In his bedroom when Riley'd taken his coat off? But surely Christian would've mentioned it.

No. No, it was somewhere on the street between his house and Christian's. Broken. Lost. Just like the last six years of their friendship.

CHAPTER
Seven

MITCH GREYSON'S HOUSE WAS NOT AT ALL WHAT Christian expected. A left-winger on Toronto's first line, Mitch was such an elitist in interviews that Christian thought his home would reflect his personality. To his surprise, Christian actually found himself liking the guy. Mitch really wasn't all that bad in person. The TV cameras must make him nervous, or maybe the journalists or reporters or something because he was a complete douche nozzle on air. But in person he resonated warmth and friendship and a certain strength he lacked on TV. Turned out Mitch's home did reflect his personality, just not in the way Christian was expecting. Instead of an enormous, pretentious McMansion, he had a charming, semidetached, late nineteenth century Richardsonian Romanesque home in Toronto's Annex neighborhood. It wasn't huge, yet it was large enough to easily host half the hockey team and their partners on New Year's Eve.

The party spilled out into the backyard, where several outdoor heaters kept the crowd warm. He and Riley stayed inside. Christian kept seeking Riley out in the crowd, as if he'd disappear if Christian didn't keep an eye on him. He was across the room right now, speaking quietly with his old goaltending coach. He caught Christian's eye and winked when the coach wasn't looking.

It was cool that Riley's former teammates still kept in touch with him even though Riley hadn't played with them for two years. It showed the kind of person Riley was, the kind of friend he was. Made Christian proud to know him. On the drive here Riley had mentioned that though he hadn't been out publicly while playing, he was out to his teammates, coaches, and the team's general manager. What was clear in the way Riley's friends interacted with him was that none of them gave a shit he was gay.

"Okay, I know this might be a stupid question." Mitch reappeared at Christian's side and offered him his second beer of the night. Christian didn't particularly want it, but it seemed rude to refuse, so he took it. He'd just have to nurse it slowly so he wasn't hammered later, in case he was the one who had to drive home. "What does a digital marketer do?"

For some reason, Mitch had glommed onto Christian when he and Riley had first arrived and hadn't let him go since. It was flattering and yet kind of weird. Mitch was a good-looking guy: an inch or two shorter than Christian's own six feet, fit, curly brown hair, light brown eyes, strong jaw covered in what appeared to be a permanent five o'clock shadow. He wasn't flirting so much as feeling Christian out. For what, Christian had no idea, but whatever it was, it wasn't sexual. Yeah Christian's gaydar might be blowing up like Times Square at midnight, but Mitch wasn't angling for a hookup. There was something else he wanted. Christian wished he'd dispense with the pleasantries and just ask already. Why did people feel like they needed to beat around the bush?

"Well." Christian took a sip of his beer and thought about how best to answer that. "We do a lot of different things and some of us are really specialized. We can do anything from study analytics so we know who to target, design websites, analyze performance. We develop the best strategies to market a product or a brand—"

"You do all that?" Mitch interrupted to ask.

Christian shrugged. "Yeah."

"You design websites, too?"

"I do." It was his favorite part. Sadly, he didn't get to do much of it.

Mitch rubbed a hand along his jaw and peered at something over Christian's shoulder. "I have a...friend. An author. Whose first book—well, second. First under this pen name. Anyway." He waved a hand. "Doesn't matter. He's just been signed by an indie publishing house. They're willing to help with creating a website but the royalties they're asking for if they do are a bit ridiculous. We thought it might be better to just hire a web designer, but I get the feeling they're over-charging us in their estimates. He could do it himself, you know, one of those free ones...no?"

Christian was shaking his head. "They don't have the best platforms. Don't get me wrong, they're user-friendly and if you upgrade to a paid subscription, you get a lot more func-tionality. But unless you know what you're doing, the paid ones don't make sense. Yet if you want reach, you need some-thing more than a free one."

Mitch let out an impatient breath. "Yeah, that's what we figured."

"Here." Christian took his phone out of his pocket. "Have you seen Riley's website for Warm Glow?"

"Yeah. He doesn't have the menu on there."

Christian swallowed a chuckle. "Here's the new one I designed for him." He passed Mitch his phone. While Mitch tapped through the various pages of what was, admittedly, a very nice website with a mobile-friendly design, Christian sought Riley out and found him still in discussion with his old coach on the other side of the room.

Earlier, when they'd arrived, Riley had introduced Mitch to Christian with a "This is the guy you're looking for." Chris-tian hadn't paid any attention at the time because he was in a room full of hockey players. *Toronto* hockey players. *His* team. His and Riley's team. They'd gotten never-ending grief from their parents for not being Montreal fans, but when they were small Montreal had seemed so far away.

He wasn't ashamed to admit it: He was totally starstruck.

Sometimes he forgot that Riley had played with these guys. He hadn't been kidding when he told Riley that hockey players were celebrities in Canada. But to him, Riley was just...Riley.

"Can you do something like this for an author?" Mitch handed him back his phone. "All interactive and clean and nice and—" He gestured at the phone. "—that?"

Ten minutes later Christian had a potential first client for the freelance web design business he hadn't even known he wanted. Second client if you counted Riley, which Christian didn't seeing as Riley wasn't paying him. In fact, Christian had forked over the money for his website upgrades himself.

But whatever. His first client!

Potential client.

Right, right. He still had to meet with Mitch's author friend, provide an estimate. But still. If it proved fruitful, it might be a sign it was time to become his own boss.

THIS PARTY WAS SUCH A TYPICAL HOCKEY PLAYER PARTY, Riley had to laugh. The WAGs—wives and girlfriends—sat together on the couches in the living room drinking champagne and munching on finger foods. There was a group of players huddled around the food in the kitchen as if they expected it to disappear at any moment. A few guys were watching the Pittsburgh vs Buffalo game in one room, and others were playing *NHL 17* on the PlayStation in another.

More than one ex-teammate had given Riley shit for not keeping in better touch.

Truth was he'd found it too hard to be around these guys after his injury. Knowing they still had the ability to play professionally and that he'd never get to do so again? Those first couple of months after he got hurt weren't exactly shining moments for him and he'd pulled further and further away from his friends. Once he'd finally gotten over his whole woe-is-me funkitude, he'd been so embarrassed at his own behavior that he still hadn't reached out to his teammates.

He was emotionally mature like that.

But they hadn't given up on him. Not once, as much as he would've liked them to in the beginning.

Man, it was great being in the same room with these guys again. As much as he loved Warm Glow and working with Sam, he missed hockey. Missed the feeling of family being part of a team gave him.

"How's the bakery treating you, Deschamps?"

Riley tuned back into the conversation he was having with his old goaltending coach. The man had been just as devastated as Riley when he'd found out Riley couldn't play anymore.

"Keeps me busy," Riley said noncommittally. He was sure the last thing Coach Davenport expected him to do once he recuperated was to open a bakery.

"Have you given any thought to what we discussed a few months ago?"

Translation: *What do you think you're doing with your life, Deschamps? If you really want to run a bakery for the rest of your life I'll stop hounding you. But is it really what you want? And think hard before you answer that.*

Coach Davenport was the type of person whose words held subtext.

"Actually, I have," Riley admitted.

Coach nodded. "Good. I have a friend who's an assistant coach for the Milton Trailblazers, an OHL team." *OHL*. The Ontario Hockey League. One of three major junior ice hockey leagues that made up the Canadian Hockey League. Riley's palms started to sweat. "They're looking for a goal-tending coach. They haven't had one in a few years and their game's starting to suffer. Is your email address still the same? I'll forward your contact info to my friend there."

Translation: *I'm going to set up an interview for you. My coaching friend will email you the details. You better show up. Don't let me down, Deschamps.*

Riley liked that Coach didn't ask if Riley wanted him to send his friend his contact info. Simply ran over him, not allowing him to say no. Not that Riley would. Not anymore. Sure, he'd needed the space from hockey for a while but two years was enough. He was ready to get back into the game. The noncompetitive rec league he was currently part of that only played a game twice a month was all well and fine. But it didn't fill that part of him that needed the adrenaline rush of a hockey puck shot at him thirty times a game.

He'd loved coaching that kid on Christmas Eve, the one who'd been so bundled he could barely move his arms to shoot the puck. Yeah, the kid couldn't find the net with a compass, but he'd had heart and enthusiasm. And that was all it took for a kid to want to learn.

Trying to bank his own enthusiasm, Riley heaved a dose of reality on the conversation. "I've never coached, though. I might suck."

"You might," Coach said, not one to mince words. "And I suspect they'll give you a trial period before signing you on permanently. But you've been playing goalie since you were, what, seven? Eight? My guess is you'll be a natural."

His heart pounded at the thought of those kids—teenagers—looking to him for advice, for guidance, for instruction. Leadership. Mentorship. He'd never be able to live with himself if he let them down.

But would he regret it if he let himself down by not jumping on this opportunity?

From across the room, Christian watched Riley finish his discussion with his old coach. As soon as the other man walked away, Riley's eyes scanned the room, searching. Not finding what they were looking for until they landed on—

Him. Christian's stomach fluttered at the smile that bloomed on Riley's face. Needing to be near him, Christian said a polite "Excuse me" to Mitch and made his way over. The front door opened when he was halfway across the room and a tall, jacked dude walked in.

Holy hockey players, Batman! Eyes wide, he double-timed to Riley and clutched his arm.

"Riles," he whispered, shaking Riley's arm. "Riles."

Riley was looking at him like he had eight heads. "What?"

"That's Alex Dean."

"Yeah."

"*The* Alex Dean. One of the greatest defensemen in the history of the NHL. *Alex. Dean.*"

He was in the same room as Alex Dean. Somebody pinch him.

"He had fifty-two points last season," Christian informed Riley. "And he saw more ice time than any other defenseman in the league." Alex Dean was his hero. "Do you think he'll talk to me? No," Christian answered his own question. "No, of course he won't. He's way too cool for school."

"Who are you, right now?"

"Is he single? He was with someone for a really long time but nobody knows if that's still a thing or not."

"It is. Not that it matters," Riley growled. "He can't have you."

The possessiveness momentarily distracted Christian from Alex Dean.

"I'll introduce you if you want. Not," Riley continued, pointing a finger in his face, "so you can sleep with him.

Strictly so you can, I don't know...get his autograph? Or whatever."

"What? No! What will I say? What will I *do*?"

"Just be yourself." Riley stared at him for a second. "Okay, not *this* self." He waved a hand at Christian as if to encompass all the weirdness he was currently emitting. "This self is freaking me out a bit."

"But it's *Alex Dean*."

"No shit," Riley deadpanned.

"Did I hear my name?"

They turned at the voice and oh. Good. God. Alex Dean was even more jacked in person. And that damn scar across his eyebrow shouldn't have been hot, yet it made his face even more ruggedly handsome.

"Hey, man." Riley offered Alex Dean his hand. "How's it going?"

Christian watched as Riley chatted with Alex Dean as if they were friends. Of course, they were. How had Christian never put two and two together? They'd played on the same goddamn team.

"It's good to see you on your feet, Desie," Alex Dean said. *Desie* was the nickname somebody had given Riley years ago, when they'd played hockey in elementary school. Because apparently "Deschamps" was just too unwieldy for little anglophone kids.

"Is this your guy?" Alex Dean nodded at Christian. "The one in Vancouver?"

Riley had talked about him with *Alex Dean*? He was going to swoon.

"Alex, meet Christian. He's a huge fan, it seems."

Christian shook his hand and proceeded to vomit verbal diarrhea all over Alex Dean's perfectly clean shoes. That play against Boston? Man, that was so epic, Christian had rewound it a dozen times. And that fight with Ottawa's defenseman? Christian knew Alex'd kick his ass. And that game against Cleveland last year when he'd scored a hat trick? That was fucking awesome!

"I am so sorry," Riley said to Alex Dean, big, shocked eyes on Christian.

Alex Dean only laughed. "It's okay. It's always nice to meet a fan. It was nice to meet you, Christian. I'm going to go grab a drink. Desie, don't be a stranger."

Christian needed a drink of his own after that. He'd lost his beer somewhere. Probably set it on a table but now he couldn't remember which one. Oh well.

"That was *Alex Dean*."

Riley rolled his eyes.

"I scared him away, didn't I?" Whatever, he didn't even care. "My life is made. I can die happy now."

Chuckling, Riley grabbed his face in his hands and kissed him. With tongue. Lots of tongue. Right there in front of a dozen pro athletes and their spouses and girl-friends.

"Wanna go home now?" Riley asked. "It's eleven."

Eleven. The time they'd agreed was a hard stop. Because as much fun as it was to hang out with a bunch of hockey players, it turned out neither one of them wanted to be here. Riley came because he'd made a commitment weeks ago. Christian tagged along because he had no other New Year's Eve plans—his ultracool plans to spend the night with his mom got kiboshed when she flounced out of the house dressed to the nines to party with her friends down the street. And his less cool, extremely relaxing, yet super old-person plan to stay home alone and watch the ball drop on TV got nixed when Riley showed up at seven thirty and told him to get dressed because they were going to a party.

Sure. Christian went. Because when one of them led, the other one followed. Just like always.

"Yes," Christian said. He leaned forward and pressed a quick, hard kiss to Riley's mouth. "Let's go home."

Riley's grin was so naughty Christian's dick took notice in his pants. Why couldn't the goddamn party be in Oakville? Now they'd have what was likely a forty-minute drive home before Christian could jump Riley's bones.

They wound their way through partygoers, Riley calling out goodbyes. Christian stared at his ass in front of them as they walked. And then walked into said ass when Riley stopped because he couldn't find the host to say thanks and Happy New Year.

Christian stood impatiently by, watching Riley stand on his tippy toes to peer above heads in search of Mitch. He growled in frustration when Riley put his hand on his shoulder, using Christian as extra leverage. If they didn't get going now, they'd still be on the road, stuck in the car when midnight hit. And Christian wanted to be in something else when that happened. Something named Riley. Or the other way around; he wasn't about to get picky about who did who.

"I'll just send them a text," Riley said. They finally shrugged on coats and slipped into boots and left the house.

It was quiet on the street, the only sounds the muted conversations coming from the house and his and Riley's footsteps crunching in the snow. Christian was happy to see Riley walking pain-free again. Their snowboarding day had really fucked him up.

It hurt Christian to see Riley in pain and it hurt that there wasn't anything he could do to help. And it hurt him that Riley couldn't play anymore, not professionally at least. All that hard work flushed down the drain because a lunatic on skates hadn't stopped before crashing into him.

Riley's car was parked on the street right in front of the house—primo parking in The Annex. They'd gotten here early (so they could leave early) and lucked out.

"I'll drive," Riley said. "I haven't had anything to drink."

"No?" Christian opened the passenger side door. Riley walked around the car to the other side. "What were you drinking?"

"Ginger ale."

How come no one had offered him ginger ale?

A sound pierced the night. A quiet chuckle so unexpected on the deadened street it made Christian turn. There, on the side of Mitch's house, Christian could barely make out two forms. They were hidden by the dark, but the street light was bright enough that he could see the puckered scar on the taller one's face—the one leaning against the side of the house—and the curly hair of the shorter one, who was tucked into the V of the jacked one's legs.

Holy shit! He all but flew into the car.

"Riles!"

Something in his tone must've alerted Riley because the man paused in the act of putting on his seatbelt to look at him warily.

"I swear to God, if this is about Alex Dean again..."

"I just saw him making out with Mitch Greyson on the side of the house!"

Clicking his seatbelt into place, Riley snorted and started the car.

"You don't believe me?"

"Oh, I believe you. It's just old news. Well, old to me anyway."

Christian blinked at him. "I don't know what that means."

Riley's smile was gently amused and he reached out to put his hand around Christian's neck. "T. Babe. They're married." He kissed Christian's cheek before pulling away from the curb.

Married? The giant, jacked defenseman and the asshole left-winger who was actually a closeted nice guy?

"Wow. That is so much jerk off fodder."

"Hey!" Riley protested, laughing. "What am I? Chopped liver?"

"Aw, Riley, honey, never." Christian squeezed his guy's thigh. "You're not liver. You're the steak to my mashed potatoes."

Riley navigated out of The Annex and onto Spadina, heading south toward the Gardiner Expressway. Somewhere in the middle of Chinatown he must've felt Christian's stare because he looked over briefly before returning his attention to the road.

"Oh! That was you trying to be funny."

Trying?

Christian sighed and rested his head against the headrest. "My brand of humor is lost on you."

They made it home faster than they should've owing to the lack of cars on the roads. Apparently, everyone was already at the parties they needed to be at. They drove mostly in a contented silence, each of them ignoring the giant Rocky Mountain-sized elephant in the car named Christian Flies Back to Vancouver in Three Days.

Two and a half days actually, seeing as his flight was midmorning on the third. But fuck it. He wasn't going to think about that tonight. Wasn't going to think about how much it would suck to get on that plane. Wasn't going to think about how it would hurt so bad to go back to being just friends with Riley.

He wasn't any closer to figuring out what Riley wanted than he had been a week and a half ago. They'd fallen into their old rhythms and patterns, like they'd never been apart. But *When you go back to BC* Riley had said on Christmas Eve. The words kept bouncing around Christian's brain, making him think Riley was fine with him heading back to Vancouver in a couple of days.

Don't think about it. Right. Things he'd promised himself he wasn't going to think about. Not tonight. Tonight was for celebrating.

Christian looked over at Riley and found him with a slight smile on his face. That smile had been absent the past few days. Ever since the night Riley had noticed Christian's tattoo he'd been upset about something. But he wouldn't say much other than he'd had something that held a lot of sentimental value and he'd lost it. Whatever it was, he was sad enough that he closed himself in his bathroom that night when he thought Christian was asleep and cried softly. He was still sniffly when he came back to bed and Christian had been at a loss. All he could do was hold Riley until he fell asleep. It was only this morning that he'd finally snapped out of his funk.

They were off the highway now, driving south on Trafalgar toward home. There were hardly any other cars on the road. With the threat of crashing minimized and with only minutes left until they pulled into Riley's driveway, Christian took the opportunity to do what he'd wanted to do since Riley showed up at his door hours earlier.

Unbuckling his seatbelt, ignoring Riley's "What are you doing?" he reached over and unzipped Riley's jeans.

"Jesus!" Riley's hips thrust up when Christian dug into his underwear to palm him. He was already half hard. "Are you trying to get us killed?"

"With pleasure, maybe."

Riley rolled his eyes. Even Christian could admit that was a bad joke.

"What if we run into RIDE?" Riley asked.

Christian leaned over the console and took Riley's dick out of his underwear. RIDE. The Reduce Impaired Driving Everywhere program. They'd be out in force tonight. Christian was surprised they hadn't come across one yet.

"Give me a heads up if we do," he said to Christian. "Kind of like your head is up." He gave Riley's dick a waggle.

"Oh my God." Riley groaned. "Your jokes are getting worse as the night goes—oh, fuck!" He interrupted himself to swear when Christian bent to suck Riley's now-hard dick into his mouth.

Riley was warm and salty. Christian ran his tongue along the underside of Riley's cock head, licking up pre-come as it came dribbling out. He used one hand to hold Riley's dick steady. The other squeezed Riley's balls.

Riley swore like a sailor. Christian could feel the twists and turns of the car, which meant they must be almost home. A thought that was confirmed when the car stopped and Riley's hands fisted in Christian's hair.

"T. Shit." He seemed incapable of more words.

Now that they were stopped, Christian opened up his throat, allowing Riley all the way in, knowing that this would do it for him. He hummed, and Riley came into his throat with a moan, one hand still in Christian's hair, the other squeezing the steering wheel.

Christian licked Riley clean, then tucked his softened dick back into his underwear and zipped up his jeans like nothing had happened.

Except Riley was panting and sweating and his eyes were glazed. He turned to look at Christian. "How horny are you right now?"

Was that a trick question? Christian glanced down at the dick in his own pants that was trying to make an escape then to Riley's dazed expression. "I just blew you in the car," he said by way of explanation.

Riley chuckled. "Come on."

Inside the house, they left their coats and boots by the front door. Riley headed down the hall toward the bedroom. Christian admired his backside: broad shoulders, tapered waist, goalie ass, muscled thighs. Christian rearranged his dick in his boxer briefs to alleviate the pressure. Hopefully, they'd be getting naked any second. There was only fifteen minutes until midnight, and they'd vowed to ring in the New Year by making metaphorical fireworks in bed. He felt heated from the inside and little tingles of electricity spread upward from his balls.

Halfway to the bedroom, Riley turned, his smile wide and wicked, "You want to take me right here, don't you?"

Christian couldn't do anything but nod. Riley walked backward toward the bedroom, eyes on Christian's. He was hard again, probably as hard as Christian, who hadn't had the luxury of an orgasm yet.

Riley beckoned him with a finger. "Coming?"

Yes. Hopefully in more ways than one.

Lured by some invisible force between them, Christian trailed after Riley, following him into the bedroom. Riley took off his sweater and all that bared skin broke something in Christian. Rushing forward, he pulled Riley to him and slanted his mouth over Riley's in a kiss that started out hot and just kept heating. He lifted one of Riley's legs around his hip and tumbled them onto the bed, landing on top of Riley. He wanted to take his time with Riley but something was making him rush. Something created a sense of urgency that only served to remind him he'd be gone soon.

Riley didn't seem to mind his pace. His hands found their way into Christian's pants and underneath his underwear to squeeze his ass. Christian moaned into Riley's mouth. Riley tasted like sugar, like sex. Like Riley.

Christian's legs were tangled in the pants and underwear Riley was desperately trying to remove and he couldn't help but rest his forehead on Riley's shoulder and chuckle.

"What?" Riley asked, out of breath.

"Just us." They were so hot for each other Christian didn't doubt they'd be willing to rip at clothes to get naked.

Riley's hands swept up Christian's back, taking his T-shirt with it. Everything in Riley froze then as he cupped Christian's T necklace in the palm of his hand. For some reason, every time he saw Christian wearing it, it caused his whole being to soften.

"One of these days," Christian growled, nipping Riley's chin, "you're going to tell me what it means."

"No."

"Yes." Christian kissed Riley's neck, his collarbone.

"No."

An idea formed and Christian lifted his head to look at Riley. "Can I guess? Will you tell me if I guess right?"

Riley looked intrigued by the idea and he nodded. "Okay. But you're not gonna get it."

"We'll see. Is it...tall?" He bit Riley's nipple.

Riley snorted a laugh. "No."

"Tantalizing?"

"No."

Christian pressed a fast kiss to Riley's lips. "Tasty?"

Riley was smiling at him. "No."

"Hmm." Christian made his way down Riley's chest, laved at his belly button. Riley gasped. "Trendy?"

"No. That's a good one, though. Your hairstyle's certainly trendy."

Christian stopped what he was doing to peer up at Riley with a frown. "What's wrong my hairstyle?"

"Nothing. I like it. Suits you." Riley pressed on Christian's head. "Keep doing what you were doing."

Grunting, Christian pulled Riley's pants and underwear off in one smooth motion, then reached into the night table for the lube. Spread out like this, just for him, Riley was strong and glorious. His hard dick curved up toward his belly, his balls were tight, his thigh muscles rippled. Christian knelt between his thighs and pressed a lubed thumb to Riley's hole.

"Does it stand for...tight?"

Riley sucked in a breath at the intrusion. "No."

Crouching over Riley, Christian met his eyes. "Talented?" he asked, and licked a path from Riley's balls to the tip of his dick.

"Yes," Riley said through gritted teeth, head thrown back. "Yes, that must be it."

Scissoring his lubed fingers, Christian watched Riley's hole widen. Sweat drip down his neck, between his shoulder blades. Riley moaned and spread his legs even wider, gaze meeting Christian's. With those eyes on his, Christian leaned over and licked Riley's dick from root to tip again.

"Fuck T, enough. I'm ready."

Taking him at his word, Christian lathered up his own erection with some lube. Resting one hand on Riley's abdomen, he lined himself up with Riley's hole with the other and pushed in slowly. God, Riley was tight and perfect and his body took his like they were meant to be. Straightening up, he rested his hands on Riley's thighs and started to pump.

"Riles..."

"Yeah, yeah, yeah." Riley chanted in time with Christian's thrusts. He held out a hand and grabbed Christian's wrist. "You're too far."

Yes. Yes, he was. Leaning over, chest to chest, Christian planted his left elbow on the mattress and buried that hand in Riley's hair. The other hand gripped Riley's ass so hard he was sure he'd leave imprints. Riley's fingernails dug into Christian's lower back and the top of his ass.

Christian loomed above Riley, locking their eyes. He couldn't wait to see Riley's explode with passion. Christian continued to pump; Riley's words still kept time with Christian's thrusting.

"Fuck, yes. Fuck, yes. T...I gotta come."

"So come," Christian said, voice like rocks over gravel. Riley gripped him so good he almost lost his rhythm a couple times.

"I can't... I need..."

Yeah, Christian knew. The hand gripping Riley's ass moved to his thigh. Christian lifted it up so that Riley's knee was by his ear. The change in angle was, apparently, just enough. If he judged by Riley's howl that was.

Christian knew he was hitting Riley's prostate because it was like Riley'd been electrocuted. His whole body spasmed, nails digging into Christian's back. He squeezed his eyes shut so hard Christian automatically gentled his thrusts.

"Look at me," he said. Riley's eyes snapped to his and his hips lifted to meet Christian's. The added pressure had Christian's vision narrowing.

"Gonna come?"

"Yes," Riley whispered. And came all over their stomachs with a silent yell, mouth open, eyes wide. His squeezing ass milked Christian so hard he, too, came with a strangled curse, head buried in Riley's shoulder.

Still panting, Riley dug a hand into Christian's hair and lifted Christian's head to bring his mouth to his own. What followed was a kiss so heart-wrenchingly beautiful, Christian felt his stomach leap. Riley was calming him with this kiss, gentling him. He was speaking with this kiss and even though Christian was afraid to hope, afraid to let himself believe, he thought maybe this was Riley's way of telling him without words that he was wanted.

"Happy New Year," Christian said when they pulled apart.

"Happy New Year, T."

Christian kissed him again with all of the foolish hope in his heart.

CHAPTER
Eight

IT WASN'T UNTIL CHRISTIAN POKED HIM IN THE SHOULDER that Riley woke and realized his phone was pinging like crazy.

Christian groaned and hid his face under the covers. "Make it stop."

Too half-asleep to be amused by him, Riley reached for his phone on the nightstand to silence it.

A quiet knock at his front door.

What the fuck? What time was it anyway?

Figuring the knocking had something to do with the texts, he cracked an eye open and then abruptly closed it against the phone's glare. Jesus, it was only three thirty in the morning. What the hell was the emergency? He braved a second peek at his phone.

I'm at your front door.

Open up.

I need your mixer.

Helllloooooooooooo?

I don't have all day!

Also it's cold. Come let me in.

Sam. Needed his mixer. In the middle of the night. There was obviously something he wasn't getting.

Rubbing the sleep out of his eyes, he reluctantly crawled out of his warm bed and yanked on the first items of clothing his hand came into contact with on the floor. The boxers and T-shirt both turned out to be Christian's, but who cared? They smelled like him and Riley brought the collar of the T-shirt up to his nose to breathe in Christian's scent on his shuffle down the hall to answer the door.

"Fuck, it's cold!" he said by way of greeting.

"Good morning to you, too." Sam breezed right in, smiling sunnily as if it wasn't oh-my-God too early. "Where's your mixer?"

"Where's *your* mixer?" Riley countered, cranky with the woken-in-the-middle-of-the-night blues. He closed the door behind her.

The look she gave him was wholly unimpressed. "In my car. I need extra ones at the shop today so I can make extra bread for the two-for-one sale. We talked about this. Remember?"

He quite clearly did not. "Why did we decide to do this the day after New Year's Day?"

"It was your idea."

Was it? There was probably something witty he could say here, but he was too tired to banter and all he wanted was to get back into bed with Christian.

"Don't you need extra ovens if you're making all that extra dough?" he asked as he headed down the hall.

"That would be nice." Sam followed behind him. "But since I can't conjure more space in the kitchen for an extra oven, I'm going in an hour early. Where are you going?"

"My mixer's in the basement." He opened the basement door and started down.

"Why?" Sam called to his retreating back.

"I've never used it," he called over his shoulder. "Wouldn't even know how," he muttered to himself.

Fuckity fuck, it was nut-chillingly cold down here. The concrete floor was frigid under his bare feet. Goosebumps rose all over his body. Even his eyeballs were cold. Shoulders hunched, arms wrapped around himself, he headed for a corner called Crap I'll Never Use. Sadly, his old hockey gear was in that corner, but if everything worked out like he hoped he might be pulling it out again soon.

He found the mixer box easily and lugged it up the stairs. It was one of those five-quart, ten-speed countertop mixers. His Grandma Geneviève thought he needed one since he owned a bakery. He hadn't had the heart to tell her that he did none of the baking.

He set the box next to Sam's boots by the front door, where she wasn't waiting impatiently like he expected. Instead he found her in his living room, perusing through his new memory scrapbook.

"This is so great," she said. "Did your mom make this for you?"

"No. Christian." He wasn't sure how he felt having her look at something so personal.

Two thin blonde eyebrows went up. "Really?" Sam knew all about Christian. Probably knew their history better than Riley himself. "Wow, Riley... He must love you so much."

The way she said it—all soft and sure and sentimental—had a knot forming in his throat. "What makes you say that?"

"Well." She ran a hand through her short pixie cut. "Two reasons. First... I mean, *look* at this. It's huge." It was. Riley hadn't even finished going through it yet. "He must've started this when you were kids. You can tell how old it is just by looking at the pages. The earlier ones are yellower, there's more wear. The cover is starting to tear in the corners, here and here." Riley sat next to her on the couch. "And second... Okay, I really don't mean to drudge up a past I'm sure you and Christian have put to bed, but... Had somebody done what you did to me, disappearing after sleeping together the night after my dad's funeral?" Riley couldn't meet her eyes. Yes, he and Christian had put that to bed, but it didn't mean he wasn't still ashamed of what he'd done. "I would've burned this damn thing."

Riley wanted to laugh but found he couldn't. "Guys don't

really burn their ex's things," he said to throw some levity into the conversation.

Sam rolled her eyes. "Then if I were a guy I would've done whatever guys do... Piss on it? Anyway, the point is not only did he not burn it, he *added* to it." She flipped to the end, where there were a few blank pages waiting for Riley to fill them, and worked her way backward until she came to the last entry. "He has an actual newspaper article on the opening of Warm Glow. From October. Of this year. Not an internet printout. But an article cut out of the newspaper. How did he get this? Pretty sure the *Oakville Beaver* doesn't mail to people who live in BC. So that means, what? His subscription goes to his mom's house...and she either mails it to him every day—which would be stupid and expensive—or she keeps them for him to read when he comes back to visit?"

No. Knowing Christian, he would've told his mom to keep the issues that mentioned Riley.

"God, Riley, you're so lucky. To have someone like this in your life who knows you and loves you and who's there for you. Even if you didn't know it at the time."

Her words made his nose and eyes burn. All the shame and guilt about how he'd left things with Christian six years ago curdled in his stomach. He'd been operating the past two weeks as if those six friendless years between them hadn't happened. As if he hadn't fucked up. But he had. And when they'd talked about it on Christmas Eve it had cleared the air between them but it hadn't addressed their future or where they were going or what would happen after tomorrow.

"He goes back to Vancouver tomorrow," Riley whispered, stomach hollow.

"Does he want to?"

"I don't know. I don't think so." Because Christian hadn't mentioned it and Riley hadn't asked and he just didn't *know*.

He kept telling himself Christian was going back, wanted to go back, so that when he eventually did it wouldn't hurt as much.

"Do you want him to?"

Sam's understanding voice wasn't doing anything for his emotional stability. He looked away so she wouldn't see his chin wobble. "I don't know what to do to get him to stay," he admitted.

"Have you tried asking? Or—and I know you have a life here and everything—but you could always move there. To be together. If that's what you want."

He wanted to be together so much his entire being yearned for Christian. Even though they weren't currently in the same room, Riley knew without looking that Christian was lying in bed in Riley's room down the hall, half awake, just waiting for Riley to come back.

Had Christian waited in bed that morning six years ago, too? Waiting for Riley to come back? Only to realize, hours later, that he wasn't? That Riley was already on his way back to Denver?

His chest felt like someone was using it as a hockey net, catching the hundreds of hard pucks being shot at him until he couldn't breathe. Riley was really no good with feelings. Having them, talking about them. Christian knew that. In fact, it had been Christian who started any discussion about feelings for...well, pretty much their whole lives.

Yet Christian had also started the last one. When he'd insinuated that he was ready to give up everything, his whole life in Vancouver, to move to Denver to be with Riley. *Subtly* insinuated, as if feeling Riley out. And Riley had ran.

Now, all of a sudden, Riley had an amazing coaching opportunity fall in his lap. With a team that, quite frankly, could use his expertise if the videos he'd watched online were anything to go by. How the fuck had he been put in this situation again where he had to choose between Christian and hockey? He couldn't have both; he'd already learned that lesson the hard way. *Been there, done that. Lost my guy to prove it.*

What was obvious now hadn't been so obvious in his youth: Sometimes people needed to—hell, sometimes people *wanted* to—make sacrifices to be with the person they loved. And Christian had been willing to make that sacrifice—he'd said so on Christmas Eve. What was also plain-as-day now was that Christian wasn't going to offer himself up again. Not after he'd been so burned the last time. He was so clearly waiting for Riley to make the first move for once and Riley had done nothing the past two weeks except sit on his ass and act like everything was golden.

But it wasn't. The last two weeks might've been fun, might've been like old times, might've helped them reconnect...but they hadn't talked about the important stuff. Of course, Christian wouldn't open up, not after what happened last time. And since Christian was keeping mum, it meant Riley was too because he'd always followed Christian's lead when it came to talking about relationship stuff.

Their talk on Christmas Eve was muddled in confusing emotions in his head. Riley remembered asking Christian if the reason he hadn't moved back home was because he thought Riley didn't want him to. And he remembered Christian looking away as if he didn't want Riley to know that his opinion still meant that much to him. For the life of him Riley couldn't remember what he'd said or done after that. Had he talked his way around the topic? Was that when he'd burst into tears? Had he specifically told Christian that he'd never wanted this for them? That he missed him every day and was dying for him to come home?

Riley didn't think so. Not that it mattered anymore. Because things were going to change. Starting today.

RILEY'S SECOND COACHING OPPORTUNITY IN AS MANY DAYS came via email from Coach Davenport. Sitting on a barstool in Warm Glow's kitchen after the kind of day Riley would like to relegate to the sixth circle of hell, he gave it a quick read and silently thanked his lucky stars the coach had been at Mitch and Alex's party on New Year's Eve. The phone beeped in his hand. *Low battery 15%.* He closed out of his open apps, slipped the phone back into his pocket, then let his forehead fall to the countertop.

"I still don't understand how I didn't have enough bread," Sam said. Her voice sounded dazed and when Riley rolled his head to the side to look at her, pressing his cheek into the counter, he saw that she looked dazed, too.

Henry sat on a barstool next to Riley. "That was the busiest day we've had yet." How was it that the seventy-year-old looked fresh as a fucking daisy yet he and Sam looked like they'd just completed a bag skate, the dreaded of all hockey drills? "Did you put an ad out?"

"No," Riley muttered. How did one go about placing ads anyway? And where would he place them?

"Are you sure?" Sam asked.

Of course he was sure but he understood where they were coming from. The only advertising he'd done was to place a sign in the window. *January 2, all bread loaves buy 1 get 1 50% off!* Yet they'd been slammed all day. A small window sign shouldn't have drawn in that many people.

The bakery's front door opened and closed. Both Sam and Henry looked at him.

"Did you forget to lock the door again?" Sam asked, a heavy dose of exasperation in her voice.

Heaving a great sigh, Riley took his tired feet and aching

knee toward the front. "You two go home," he said. "You've been here longer than me."

He'd be left to finish cleaning the kitchen on his own since he'd sent his two part-timers home after they'd finished cleaning the front. But it was no less than he deserved since he'd slept in longer than he should've after being awakened in the middle of the night and had shown up late at the shop.

It was not Christian standing in his shop like he'd secretly hoped. A woman in her late seventies or early eighties with gray and white hair sticking out of a pink and purple knitted toque stood with a large tote over her shoulder.

"I'm so sorry," she said, glancing around at the upended chairs stacked on the tables. "You're closed, aren't you?"

"Yeah, sorry. We reopen at seven tomorrow morning."

"Darn. I was hoping to get the fresh bread from the advertisement on my way home."

She turned to leave but—

"Wait." Riley rounded the counter. "What advertisement?"

"The one in the *Beaver*." She took a folded newspaper out of her giant purse. "The ad's been running for the past three days."

Right there, taking up a whole half page, was an advertisement for today's sale.

January 2, 7am to 5pm!
Buy 1 get 1 50% off any loaf of fresh bread.
Baguettes, sourdough, rye, pumpernickel, gluten-free, and many more.
And try one of our award-winning pastries while you're here or enjoy
a hot lunch.
Now serving alcohol.

That last sentence looked like it had been added as an afterthought. Warm Glow's name, logo, and address appeared, as well as a full-color photo of the inside of the shop, showing the bread and pastry displays.

Christian. Who else would know that Sam's pastries had won awards? Although how he'd found that out Riley couldn't guess.

His chest filled with warmth and he bit his lip to try and stop the silly grin that wanted to escape. "Can I keep this?" he asked the lady. It was so going in his memory scrapbook.

"Sure?" She sounded like she was questioning his sanity. *How does he not know about this ad if he works here?* was probably what was going through her head right now. She turned to leave.

"Hey, wait. If you'd like to come by tomorrow for some bread, I'll honor today's sale."

"Oh!" Her eyes lit up. "That's very sweet, but I'm afraid I won't be able to come by until after five again."

"That's fine," Riley said. "Somebody's usually here until about five thirty anyway, cleaning up. I'll set a couple aside for you. What kind would you like?"

She waved a hand in the air. "Whatever you recommend, I'm not picky. You can put it aside for Martha."

"Martha. I'm Riley."

"Well, Riley, thank you. See you tomorrow."

"You will." Though he hoped not. But if things didn't go as planned with Christian then he'd need the distraction from his broken heart.

"Happy New Year!"

"Happy New Year," he said to her retreating back. The door shut behind her and he remembered to lock it this time.

Happy New Year indeed. He was clutching the newspaper to his chest as he walked through the empty kitchen to the small office he shared with Sam, pausing to lock the back door on his way. This ad... It was just additional proof that Christian was still taking care of him. Waking the laptop, he brought up his email program to respond to Coach Davenport. Christian was leaving tomorrow, which meant he didn't have a lot of time to put things in place. Man, putting this together was like orchestrating the most complicated of hockey plays. But this one was much more important. This was a play for Christian. For their future.

This was the play of his life.

CHAPTER
Nine

Mitch Greyson's author friend who needed a new website? Was Alex Dean.

Mind. Blown.

Sitting on the couch in his mom's family room, Christian still couldn't believe it. He had a copy of Alex Dean's as-of-yet unpublished gay romance on his e-reader to read on the flight to Vancouver tomorrow. Because he needed to know his client's brand before he could start designing a website for him, right?

Sure. But really, he just wanted to read *Alex Dean's book*. His gay romance book anyway, that he was publishing under a pen name. Christian had already read *No Guts, No Glory*, Alex's non-fiction bestseller about the dark side of sports that he'd published a few years ago.

"I want to read it, too," his mom said when he finished telling her about his morning meeting with Mitch and Alex. She sat in the armchair perpendicular to the couch with Trevor on her lap, watching the end of *Slumdog Millionaire*.

"I'm not allowed to share it."

The look she shot him was dry. "Not even with your mother?"

"I promised."

Shaking her head in mock disappointment, she went back to her movie. Christian opened up his laptop to get some work done. It had been the one stipulation when he'd asked his boss for an extra week off: that he keep an eye on his emails and get a couple hours of work done every day. He hadn't minded; it kept him busy when he wasn't with his mom or with Riley. Plus, a digital marketer never really took time off.

Eventually he switched gears to work on Riley's website user guide. *Slumdog Millionaire* ended and his mom traded out the DVD for *La La Land*. Christian waited for the opening scene to be over before he addressed her.

"Hey, Mom?"

"Hmm?" She barely took her eyes off Emma Stone dancing in the street with her friends.

"Sorry we haven't spent much time together the past couple of weeks." He was leaving tomorrow and he felt like he'd barely seen his mom he'd been so focused on Riley.

His mom snorted. "I didn't want to see you anyway."

What? "Hey!" Ouch.

"Oh, I don't mean it that way." She turned to look at him. "Do you remember the day you got here? And I sent you to Warm Glow to get bread?" She paused, waiting for him to figure out the rest.

"You knew Riley would be there," he said. It was as he'd suspected: she hadn't needed bread. She'd just wanted him to find Riley.

"You've missed your friend for so long, Christian. And every time you would come home to visit me, you would pretend like he doesn't live right around the corner." Damn. Had he tried too hard to avoid even looking in the direction of Riley's house? Was that how she'd figured it out? Moms. They saw through everything. "You need each other. It was time for you both to stop being stupid."

He snorted a laugh and quietly admitted to himself she was right. They did need each other. And they were both so, so stupid. Neither one of them had brought up the fact that Christian was leaving tomorrow, as if not mentioning it would prevent it from happening. Christian kept waiting and waiting for Riley to ask him to stay. After the past two weeks, it seemed like Riley wanted him to.

But what if he didn't? *When you go back to BC...* What if the past two weeks had been an extended one-night stand for Riley and tomorrow morning he'd once again disappear from Christian's life? His gut cramped at the thought and he swallowed hard. Forcing his mind back to his work didn't help keep him distracted from things he didn't want to think about. His mind kept drifting to Alex and Mitch. They'd been married for *six years* he'd found out this morning, which was about how long Alex had been playing for Toronto. But six years ago, Mitch had been fresh out of college and drafted by Boston. Then he'd been traded to a team on the West Coast. It was only a couple years ago that he'd coincidentally landed on the same team as his husband. So not only had they weathered the distance between them for those four years Mitch had played for a different team, but for however many years before that while Mitch attended college and Alex played for Florida.

Yet they'd made it work. And here he and Riley were, in the same town, and they couldn't manage to pull it together long enough to have an honest discussion about where they wanted to go from here.

It wasn't until over an hour later, butt numb from sitting in the same position, thighs warm from the laptop on his legs, that his mom interrupted his work to say, "This is going to be your life one day." Christian looked up to find her nodding at the TV.

It was the end of the movie, where Emma Stone's character, Mia, walks into Seb's to find her ex has finally made his dream come true and a little fantasy plays out. A what-if fantasy.

Christian got what his mom was saying. What if he got on that plane tomorrow? Would they randomly bump into each other one day, both of them living their own lives with new partners? Wondering how they'd fucked things up so much and how different their lives would be if they'd made different decisions?

He didn't want that for them. He'd extended his vacation time *for* Riley. So that they could...well, maybe not get back what they once had. There were too many empty years between them for that. But they could have something better, something stronger.

A long-distance relationship hadn't worked last time, so he had no reason to believe it would this time. He was older now. Wiser. More mature. More experienced. And they both had more money, so they could fly back and forth to see each other more often.

But not waking up next to Riley every day? Not being here for the good stuff and the bad? Having most of their conversations via text or phone or FaceTime? It felt like a fabrication of a relationship, one where they'd both get tired of the unoccupied space in bed where the other should be. Tired of constantly saying "I miss you," of scheduling calls around both their schedules. Tired of not being able to see or touch or hear the other half of your soul whenever you wanted.

And Riley *was* the other half of Christian's soul. They just fit. Always had. Like they saw each other better than anyone else. Better than they saw themselves even.

How did Barry Allen explain it on that episode of *Supergirl?* There are multiple Earths in the universe and they all occupy the same place in space. But they all vibrate at different frequencies, so they can't see each other. Theoretically, if you could run fast enough, you could create a breach and travel between the worlds.

So theoretically, if two of those worlds started vibrating at the same frequency, would they be able to see each other? Christian didn't know; the theory of the multiverse was just too damn confusing. But either way... That was him and Riley.

They vibrated at the same frequency. They saw each other. If they didn't they never would've made fast friends that first day of second grade.

Mind made up, Christian shut down his laptop and headed to his room to pack.

THE KNOCK ON HIS BEDROOM WINDOW SCARED THE PISS out of him a couple hours later. Clad in only a towel, hair still wet from his shower, he pulled the curtain aside. It was fully dark outside and the light was on in his room so he couldn't see who it was, but he only needed one guess to figure it out. Who else would knock on his window instead of his front door?

Riley must've enjoyed his view from out there because Christian heard a wolf whistle. Christian snorted and opened the window.

"You're hilarious," he said, deadpan.

Riley grinned at him. "I'm just appreciative."

He sat on the windowsill to take his boots off outside and Christian left him to it to get dressed. Christian's dick took too much notice of how good Riley smelled and he needed some distance. Otherwise he'd jump Riley before they had the conversation they really needed to have.

"I met with Mitch Greyson this morning," he told Riley from the bathroom. He didn't bother styling his hair. Just combed it back before looking around for the T-shirt he'd left in here earlier.

"Uh-huh," Riley said, distracted.

"Riles, Mitch's author friend? Is *Alex Dean*." He'd been dying to text Riley the news all day but he'd known the bakery would be busy and he didn't want to be a distraction.

"I know."

Of course the fucker knew. Just like he'd known that Mitch and Alex had been looking to hire a competent and affordable web designer who knew his shit but wouldn't charge them their firstborn just because they were rich. He probably also already knew that Christian had said yes when he'd been offered the job today, so he didn't bother telling him.

"Alex emailed me his book to read. The one that got accepted for publishing?" He shrugged into his T-shirt and left the bathroom in search of sweats. "It'll be published in—what are you doing?"

A naked Riley stood next to the bed, hands on his hips. Christian's dick went from lazing around to full attention almost instantly, tenting the front of his towel. Riley's golden skin shone in the overhead light, muscles on full display, cock jutting forward, pointing straight at Christian.

Christian's mouth went dry.

Riley looked at Christian's T-shirt and frowned. "What are *you* doing? I'm getting naked and you're putting clothes on? Strip!"

"Dude!" he whispered loudly, scandalized. "My mom's down the hall!"

"No, she's not. I passed her on my way here. It's book club night at Kathy's. Strip!"

Yeah, okay. Christian stripped. Conversation could wait. He lost his towel and T-shirt as fast you could say *Check, please!*

Riley was on him in an instant and his hands were everywhere. Christian gasped at the feel of him and Riley took advantage of his open mouth to swoop right in. He'd obviously gone home to change after work because he tasted minty and he smelled spicy and his skin was extra soft under Christian's hands. Riley turned them then walked Christian backward until he tumbled back onto the bed.

"You," Riley said, climbing on top of him, "have some explaining to do."

Christian groaned when Riley's teeth clamped onto a nipple. "What?" *More doing, less talking.*

"How did an ad for our sale..." Riley nipped his chin. "... get into the newspaper?"

Christian blinked at him. "Ghosts?"

Riley's snorted laugh made Christian smile. He kissed Christian again, softly this time, tongue invading Christian's mouth and rubbing deliciously against his.

"Thank you," he whispered, eyes sparkling.

"How'd it go?" Christian ran his hands up and down Riley's strong back, reveling in the feel of him, his warmth.

Riley snorted again and nosed Christian's T necklace out of the way to kiss his collarbone. "We ran out of bread an hour and a half before closing."

"Oh." Christian froze. "Shit, Riles, I'm sorry. I should've warned you so you had more inventory."

"No." Riley planted a quick kiss on Christian's lips and ran his hand down Christian's back to his ass. "Don't apologize. It was awesome, actually. Tiring, but awesome. Like, fifty percent of the people who came in were new customers."

"The power of advertising," Christian said.

Grunting, Riley kissed one nipple, then the other. He licked and laved his way down Christian's chest and stomach. "Now I'll show you the power of Riley."

Christian couldn't help an amused laugh. "I think we need to have a discussion about whose jokes are lamer."

Joking got pushed aside when Riley licked from Christian's balls to the tip of his cock, then swallowed him with his mouth. The wet heat of Riley's mouth had Christian sucking in a breath between his teeth. Riley pushed on his thighs, encouraging him to open up wider. Christian followed his direction. Setting a pillow behind his head, Christian shifted until he was propped up enough to watch what Riley was doing.

Stomach clenching at the sight of his dick going in and out of Riley's mouth, Christian dug his toes into the bedcover. He was breathing hard enough to hyperventilate but fuck. Riley was making him crazy. And when Riley inserted a thumb into his hole, squeezed his shaft, tongued the slit at the top, and met Christian's eyes with his own... Christian lost it, coming with a groan, arms flung over his head, hands fisted in his pillow.

He was still trying to draw breath when Riley crawled up his body, kissing everything in his path until he reached Christian's lips. Christian tasted himself in Riley's mouth. When Riley's mouth left his, it trailed to his ear, where Riley whispered, "I'm gonna make you come again."

The naughty words said in Riley's sexed-out throaty voice had Christian's softened dick twitching.

"Jesus," he groaned. "If this is the thanks I get for placing an ad I should do that more often."

Chuckling, Riley reached into the night table for the lube. Christian swatted at the hand Riley was using to hold himself up with and Riley fell on top of him with an "Oof!" Christian grunted at the sudden weight on his chest and buried both hands in Riley's hair, bringing Riley's face close to his.

Riley raised an inquiring eyebrow.

"Just wanted to feel you," Christian explained. Their legs were tangled, groins pressed together, but he'd wanted every part of Riley touching him.

The corners of Riley's eyes crinkled when he smiled at Christian like that, like he was amazed by him. Christian's chest went tight at the look. It only served to solidify the decision he'd made earlier.

They stayed like that for a while, Riley on top, Christian pliant beneath him. Riley's erection nudged his stomach but

Riley didn't speed things along, just stayed pressed against Christian, running his hands over Christian's body like Christian was doing to him. Sharing lazy kisses and painless nips and gentle touches.

Christian's heart fluttered and his breath stuttered at the feelings of hope and happiness stirring inside him. This. This was why a long-distance relationship would never work. He needed Riley's gasps of pleasure, his warm eyes, his caresses, his ready smile, his passionate nature, his good humor. Every. Single. Day.

Lazy kisses eventually turned heated. Questing hands gripped and clung. Christian's cock woke to half hard and when Riley lubed up a couple of fingers and slid them inside him, it went fully erect.

Christian was still slightly stretched from their languid morning sex so he didn't need much prepping. Riley only did the bare minimum before slathering his cock in lube and pressing into Christian with an amazing amount of patience considering he hadn't come yet. Riley's length felt amazing, gliding along all of Christian's nerve endings. Pleasure overcame Riley's face, the flush creeping up his chest, his mouth dropping open. Riley's whole body shuddered and when he opened his eyes, he met Christian's with a sly smirk.

Fuck, the man was sexy. Sweat glistening his skin, pupils dilated, hands clenched on Christian's thighs. Christian met Riley's smile with one of his own and shimmied down a bit, impaling himself even further on Riley's dick. Riley's smirk disappeared and he grunted, squeezing his eyes closed. Then, like a switch flipped from take-it-easy to slap shot-fast, he started to pump. Christian met him thrust for thrust, ankles hooked together at the top of Riley's ass as Riley knelt between Christian's thighs. Christian's position propped on the pillow gave him a good view of Riley's wet cock ramming in and out of him. He groaned at how erotic it was to see them like that and let his head fall back. The only sound in the room was their grunts and the *slap slap slap* of flesh hitting flesh.

Riley leaned forward and braced a hand on Christian's belly. The move had Riley's dick hitting Christian's prostate and his legs shook with the pleasure. Using his other hand, Riley jacked Christian's dick.

Christian's balls drew tight and he came groaning Riley's name, heels digging into Riley's ass. Come spurted on his stomach. Riley came in the next second, nails leaving imprints in Christian's thighs, muscles straining. Christian unlocked his ankles from around Riley and let his feet drop to the bed. Riley rested a sweaty forehead on Christian's upraised knee.

"Fuck, T," he whispered, voice wretched.

Christian chuckled. "Yeah," he said, sighing. "Yeah."

Riley's eyes met his and they grinned stupidly, lost in a post-orgasmic haze. Christian hissed when Riley pulled out gently and watched him cross the room to the bathroom to clean up.

Christian let his eyes close. He didn't normally get sleepy after sex, but his irregular schedule the past two weeks coupled with a middle-of-the-night wakeup call this morning added to remnant jet lag had his eyes struggling to stay open.

Riley came back and cleaned him up before climbing onto the bed. After much shimmying and quiet giggles, they managed to get underneath the bedcovers. On their sides facing each other, Christian tucked his face in Riley's neck and let his eyes close. Bliss. This was bliss.

"T?"

Christian meant to answer, but sleep overcame him instead.

CHAPTER
Ten

CHRISTIAN WOKE UP ALL ALONE HOURS LATER. IT WAS SO familiar it felt like a backhand shot to the sternum, the force of it bruising his insides. Forcing himself not to panic, he turned the light on to look for a clue...a shirt Riley left behind, a forgotten sock, a text, a note. Hell, a fucking smoke signal.

Nothing. It was six in the goddamn morning, still pitch black out, and Riley was already gone.

The pain of that caused needle-sharp pinpricks of ice to rake his chest. A sob caught him by surprise and he pressed the heels of his palms to his eyes.

Riley didn't want him. Nothing would take that pain away. Not after last night. Last night had been sweet and sensual yet deliciously hot and he'd thought... He'd thought it was Riley showing him how he felt about him. He thought it was Riley showing him that he was loved and wanted.

Instead it had been...Riley saying goodbye? Had Christian been right? Had the last two weeks been an extended one-night stand for Riley?

What was wrong with Christian that Riley had snuck out on him again without a word? What had he done that was so bad it made Riley not want to be with him? All Christian wanted was to move into Riley's house—even if it was haunted—and love him and cherish him and take care of him and make a life together. Why did the person he wanted most in the world not want him back?

Christian flipped onto his stomach and buried his head in Riley's side of the pillow, inhaling Riley's spicy scent. The sheets on his side of the bed were still sort of warm. Had he *just* missed Riley sneaking out? The lost opportunity had him clutching his stomach.

His throat hurt so much from holding back tears that he gave in and let them fall, crying quietly into his pillow so he didn't wake his mom.

Twice. Twice now his overwhelming hope had crushed him. Three times if he counted that summer he broke up with Riley, when he'd waited here so patiently for him to come home from school only to find out Riley was staying in Colorado for hockey camp. Was that why Riley had left? Maybe he, like Christian, was afraid of what a long-distance relationship would mean for them. But it wouldn't *be* long-distance. Christian was staying. If only he'd told Riley that last night instead of letting Riley distract him with kisses and sex.

God, he was tired. So, so tired. Emotionally drained, physically exhausted.

His mom was driving him to the airport in a bit so he wiped his tears and took a quick shower. If the warm water mixed with the tears on his face, nobody had to know. Staring into the bathroom mirror afterward, he ignored the wet hair dripping onto his face, his red eyes, the splotchy skin, and instead focused on the T necklace around his neck. He curled a fist around it, hiding it from view. It was the most precious gift anyone had given him. He still didn't know what the T stood for—might never know—but it was proof that, at some point, Riley had cared about him.

He was tempted to take it off. Put it back in its little box, rewrap it in that delicate red felt ribbon. The one that was knotted around a miniature Eiffel Tower Riley had given him after a trip to Paris with his parents in high school. Give the box to his mom and tell her to give it to Riley next time she saw him. Or he could mail it to Riley, either from here or from Vancouver.

But if this was the only piece of Riley he could have then he was keeping it.

After packing the last of his stuff—yesterday's clothes, his toiletries—cleaning his room and taking his dirty towels to the laundry room, he did something so thoroughly pathetic it made him cringe even as he did it. He sat in the living room, on the couch that faced the window.

And waited.

But Riley never came.

He watched cars drive by, neighbors on their way to work. Joggers, dog walkers, kids on their way to the bus stop up the street, high schoolers on their way to school. Heard sirens in the distance, the sound of a fire truck's horn.

A while later, with what could only be described as a sympathetic smile on her face, his mom sat next to him.

"We should go soon," she said.

Christian checked the time on his watch. 7:30 am. His flight was in three hours and it was a half hour to the airport, more in morning rush hour traffic. They'd have to leave in the next fifteen minutes.

"Sure you don't want to stay?" his mom asked. Christian knew by *stay* she meant *move back*. Which had been the plan until this morning.

"I don't think he wants me to stay, Mom." Moving home but not being with Riley? It would be too hard. *That* was the real reason he hadn't moved back. The reason he'd never shared with Riley, even though Riley won that bet on Christmas Eve.

She bumped his shoulder gently with hers. "But I want you to stay."

The simple words broke something in him, something that was loosely tied with Riley's laughter and that delicate red ribbon Riley'd used to decorate his gift with. And to his utter embarrassment, he started to cry. In front of his mom. God.

She put her arms around him and even though he was so much bigger, he hid his tear-stained face in her neck and let the tears come. He was just so...sad. And as much as he didn't want to admit it, lonely. Maybe he should move back. This was home and his mom was here. Granted, all of his friends were in BC, but that didn't mean he wouldn't make new ones here. Even if Riley didn't want him as one.

Fed up with himself, he used his hoodie's sleeves to wipe his eyes and let out a long breath. It was shaky and wet, but the second one was steadier and he kept breathing until he wasn't so choked up anymore.

"Maybe you should go find him," his mom suggested, rubbing his back. "See what he has to say?"

So Riley could reject him to his face? No, thank you.

"I'm going to take one last pass of my room," he said. Not that he thought he'd left anything behind. He just needed to get away from her kind eyes for a minute.

In his room, he took the time this moment afforded him to pull himself together. To distract himself, he did a sweep of the bathroom for anything he'd missed. Then the dresser, the closet, the desk. He checked under the bed for the hell of it and—

A glint of metal caught his eye next to the leg closest to the window. He stood, walked around the foot of the bed and picked up the item.

Oh! It was his T necklace. The sight of it brought a lump to his throat but he swallowed past it, done with tears for the day. God, if he'd left this behind he—

Wait just a goddamn minute. He fished under the collar of his hoodie. As he suspected, his hand closed around his own necklace, the metal warm from his body heat. If he was wearing his, then who the hell did this belong to?

Was this...Riley's? It was the only explanation he could think of. Riley said that he'd had Christian's necklace custom made so it wasn't like there were a lot of these little Ts floating around.

Numb, he sat on the edge of the bed. Was this the thing of sentimental value that Riley lost last week? The thing that had bummed him out for days and made him cry alone in the bathroom?

"Christian, are you ready to go?" his mom asked from his bedroom doorway. When he didn't answer, she came in and sat next to him. "What's that?"

Wordlessly he handed her the necklace.

"Oh, pretty. Is it yours?"

Christian shook his head. "Riley gave me my own. See?" He pulled it out from under his sweater.

His mom smiled and ran her thumb over the one in her hand. Flipping it over, she brought it closer to her face and squinted. "It says your name here," she said.

Christian ripped the necklace out of her hands and brought it up to his own face. There, on the back of the T, where the horizontal line met the vertical one, was his name. Chest tingling, he brought his own necklace up to his face. Stamped onto the back: *Riley*.

Okay, what?

"I don't even know what the T stands for," he whispered past the disbelief restricting his breath.

"No?" His mom took Riley's necklace out of his hands. "If I had to guess I would say *trust*. Maybe *tender*. Because that's the way you are with him. But definitely *trust*. Riley has always been a happy person. Kind, genuine, helpful, outgoing. Lots of friends. But the only person he's ever really trusted is you."

Tender. Because that's the way you are with him. It had never been a conscious thought for Christian to treat Riley that way. And there was really no reason for it. Riley was strong. He was tough. Had a good head on his shoulders. He was put together and totally capable of taking care of himself. But there was something about his very nature that always made Christian feel soft and gentle toward him. Not that he treated Riley with kid gloves, that wasn't it at all. Just that Riley deserved to be taken care of.

Fingering the necklace around his neck, sadness and hurt morphed into anger and doubt so fast it left his head spinning. The leather string on Riley's necklace was frayed and shabby. Clearly it had been worn with much frequency for a long time. So Riley had, what? Been wearing this for years? And then just left this morning even though this necklace proved that somewhere inside of him there still existed a spot for Christian?

Oh, fuck this shit. No way was he letting Riley get away with hiding from his feelings. Not this time.

Grabbing Riley's necklace out of his mom's hand, he stood, said, "I'll be right back," took a few precious seconds to put on his boots and coat, and left the house.

The walk to Riley's threw him back in time six years. To another morning where he'd woken up alone, thinking Riley had needed to leave to go see his parents or something. Christian had waited in bed, thinking of all the things he'd need to settle in Vancouver so he could move to Denver to be with Riley. Thinking that since it was early September, still the beginning of the school year, he was probably eligible for a partial refund from UBC if he withdrew from his courses as soon as possible. The money from the refund could fund his move to Denver, where he'd live with Riley and they'd make a home together just like they'd once talked about. Once Riley got drafted by the NHL—Christian had always known that he would be—then maybe he could go back to school in whatever city they ended up in and finish his degree.

He'd been so excited to start their new life together. One he'd finally admitted to himself he wanted desperately after his dad died. His sudden death had had Christian reevaluating his priorities, and sorry UBC, but Riley came first.

Christian had dozed in bed for a couple hours. When Riley didn't come back, he got annoyed and texted him. And when that still didn't yield any results he got dressed and took this exact same walk to Riley's.

Back then Riley's mom had answered the door only to tell him that Riley was already on his way back to Denver. Didn't Riley tell Christian that he couldn't stay until the end of the week anymore? That he had to go back to school early for hockey?

Still Christian hadn't panicked even though a curl of apprehension had started unfolding in his chest. He'd simply sent Riley another text. *Call me when you land.*

Nothing. No call, no text, no email. No letter via owl. It wasn't until a few days later, when he was back at school in Vancouver, that he'd realized it was truly over.

This time around? Nobody answered Riley's door. Christian knocked again, louder. Looked through the front window for any sign of life. Nada.

Frustrated, he was halfway to Warm Glow when he paused on the sidewalk next to their frozen pond. Shit. If he didn't leave for the airport now he'd miss his flight. Digging into his pockets for his phone so he could call the airline and get on a later flight, he—

Fuck his life. He'd left his goddamn phone at his mom's. He had a brief moment of indecision where he took one step toward home then turned and took one toward Warm Glow. Then changed his mind and turned for home before changing his mind *again* and taking a step in the other direction. Basically, twirling in circles in one place, chasing his tail like a confused puppy.

The loud patter of booted feet hitting the sidewalk in what sounded like a full-out run snapped him out of it and he turned for Warm Glow at a clipped pace. A clipped pace that slowed and eventually stopped when he realized it was Riley who was running full-tilt toward him. Dressed in the same outfit he'd worn to Christian's last night—lived-in jeans and flannel shirt over a T-shirt—he waved his hand in the air when he spotted Christian and a smile split his face.

"Wait!" he yelled from ten feet away.

Seriously? Where the fuck else did he think Christian was going to go?

Riley came to a stop in front of Christian, hair a mess, breath puffing out in front of him as he tried to catch his breath. He bent over and rested his hands on his knees.

"Sorry," he wheezed. "There was...gas leak...firefighters everywhere...took forever to figure out...where it was coming from. My phone died and I couldn't...text you. Holy shit." He finally caught his breath and unbent from his folded position. "I need to drop the weights and start doing some cardio." Christian was slowly dying over here and Riley was making jokes? Annoyed with himself, with Riley, with the world in general, Christian growled low in his throat, fisted two hands in Riley's flannel, and went in for the good morning kiss he'd desperately wanted to wake up to. Riley kissed him back as if he'd desperately wanted it too. One of his hands buried itself in Christian's hair. The other fisted Christian's coat at his lower back, bringing their bodies flush. Christian groaned at the taste of Riley and continued kissing him while morning commuters drove past—ignoring one obnoxious honk—and dog walkers walked by with their charges.

It wasn't until one particularly yappy poodle pawed at his leg that Christian pulled back, hands remaining on Riley's back. Riley's face was flushed, his eyes glowed, and his smile...

It put every doubt Christian had to rest. He swore he could literally *feel* the tension bleeding from his body.

Riley's cold hands framed Christian's face. "Can you delay your flight until later? I haven't had a chance to book my ticket yet."

Christian shook his head but it didn't help with the confusion clouding his brain. "Huh?"

"I'm coming with you." Riley's smile dimmed somewhat. "I said so before I left this morning. Remember?"

Christian was shaking his head.

"I got the text from Sam," Riley explained, sounding unsure. "You woke up as I was getting dressed. I told you to go back to sleep and to not leave for the airport without me 'cause I was coming with you. And you...grunted." Realization tinged his voice and he chuckled softly. "And went back to sleep. Yeah, you don't remember that at all, do you?"

Christian was still shaking his head, Riley's smile doing funny things to his chest that made him smile back.

"So...where were you going just now?"

Christian reached into his pocket. "I was coming to ask about this." He handed Riley the necklace.

"You found it!" Riley's wet eyes didn't surprise Christian one bit. "Where was it?"

"Under my bed," Christian said. Riley slipped it over his head, the T glinting metallic against his black T-shirt. Christian traced the T with a finger. "You've had this a long time."

"Bought it at the same time I bought yours," Riley admitted, swallowing roughly. "It was supposed to be your present for our fifth anniversary but..."

But Christian had broken up with him a few months earlier. And Riley had kept the necklaces this whole time. It reminded Christian of the stack of birthday and Christmas gifts he had for Riley in his closet in Vancouver.

"T," Riley said, his eyes snagging Christian's, hands back

on Christian's face. "There hasn't been a day that's gone by since we broke up that I haven't thought about you." His voice wobbled yet he kept going. "Wondered where you were and what you were doing and if you were still watching *Supernatural*. Or what you had for breakfast and if it was the same thing I had. If you were happy."

Christian's own eyes watered and he leaned his forehead against Riley's.

"Please let me come with you," Riley whispered, breath ghosting over Christian's lips.

"Riley, honey." Christian leaned back an inch to look Riley in the eye. "I'm staying."

"Oh." Riley's eyes swam with confusion until he seemed to realize what Christian had said. "Oh! Okay. Wow. Okay. But I had everything all planned," he said, earnest. "I have a job ad out for a manager for Warm Glow and...and...and my bag is packed and ready to go, and my neighbor... She's going to check my mail for me and I even have a job interview lined up for next week!"

"Riles, wait, slow down." Christian took Riley by the waist and shook him slightly. "What job interview?" Because if it was something Riley really wanted then that was something they needed to consider.

"Oh, I asked Coach Davenport to see if there were any coaching opportunities in Vancouver. Apparently there's a team in...White Rock?...that needs an assistant coach." Riley shrugged. "Could've been fun."

Riley didn't seem all that enthused about it. Christian narrowed his eyes on him. "But?"

"But..." Riley looked away, fingers playing with the zipper on Christian's coat. "Um, there's a job opening with the Milton Trailblazers. For a goaltending coach."

A goaltending coach. For an OHL team located a thirty-minute drive away. It was so perfectly right for Riley. Christian's heart leapt, thrilled that Riley was finally ready to let hockey into his life again.

"And you were just going to what?" Christian asked, incredulous. "Pass up that opportunity to move to BC with me?"

When Riley lifted his head those ocean blue eyes were more serious than Christian had ever seen them. "I chose hockey over you once, T. I didn't mean to, but I did. I'm never doing that again. I love you and wherever you go I go too from now on."

Christian let out a shaky breath that ended in a quiet chuckle. "Okay. Come here." He pulled Riley to him and buried his face in Riley's neck. "I love you, too." Riley was warm and here and everything. Everything in Christian's life had led them to this moment. "Scared me when you weren't there this morning."

Riley held him tighter. "I'm sorry," he whispered against Christian's neck.

"Cancel that interview in BC. Set one up with the Milton team," Christian said.

He felt Riley's smile against his skin. "Yeah?"

"Yeah."

"'Cause you're staying."

"Yeah, Riley, honey, I'm staying." Except... "Um." He pulled out of the hug. "Actually, I do sort of need to get on a plane today." He wasn't a nice enough person to say that the panic in Riley's eyes didn't make him feel really fucking awesome. Because it totally, definitely did. "I'm coming back," he promised. "But I do need to get back to work to hand in my notice and pack up my stuff and lease my apartment."

"Oh," Riley said, then kissed him hard and fast. "That's okay, then. So you'll be back in, what? A week?"

"In what fantasy universe does moving only take a week?"

Riley shrugged. "I don't know. How much stuff do you have there? And it's not like you need to look for a place to live. You know you're moving in with me."

"Only if you find a priest or an exorcist or a witch or something to clear out those ghosts. Hell, I'll even take smudging."

Riley laughed and Christian couldn't help but marvel at how he'd have that sound in his life from now until forever.

"Deal," Riley said. "Anything else?"

Christian eyed the frozen pond to his right. At some point in the next few minutes he'd have to call the airline to reschedule his flight for later in the day, but after that?

"Feel like a game before I leave?"

Grinning, Riley linked their fingers together and turned them in the direction of his house so they could grab some gear. When Riley shivered, Christian let his hand go to put his arm around him, letting Riley huddle into his side.

"Remind me to grab a coat," Riley said.

"You're lucky there's no windchill today." Christian ran his hand along Riley's upper arm. "Why aren't you wearing one anyway?"

"I was in a hurry. Had to get to you."

Christian smiled and kissed the top of Riley's head, letting that thought settle securely into his bones as he walked home with his guy.

EPILOGUE

RILEY HESITATED. THE BIG, WHITE DOOR BLOCKING HIS entry into Christian's Vancouver apartment loomed ominously in front of him, a wall that said "You can't have him!"

Or maybe that was his insecurities talking.

His phone went off in his pocket, an obnoxiously loud hockey goal horn. Christian.

Packing is finally fucking done. Fuck, who knew I had so much fucking stuff?

Three F-bombs in only two sentences. Even for Christian that was a lot. He must really be sick and tired of packing. The phone buzzed in his hand before Riley could type a reply.

I can't fucking wait to see you.

Definitely his insecurities.

According to Riley's research, the quickest drive from Vancouver to Oakville was through the northern United States. *Quickest* being relative, at only 40 hours of driving time, not including food and pee breaks and sleep.

Which meant if Christian left tomorrow like he was planning, he'd arrive in Oakville in, oh, about way-too-damn-long-for-Riley's-sanity.

Riley wasn't having it, which was how he'd found himself here late on a Sunday afternoon in early February: in Vancouver, outside Christian's apartment. It'd been over four weeks —thirty-two whole days but who was counting?—since they'd seen each other. He couldn't take another day.

Yet, for some reason, he hesitated before knocking on the door. Four weeks ago, Riley had thought that Christian's move to Oakville would only take a week. Fast forward to the present and the delays in Christian's move had Riley questioning whether his boyfriend actually did want to move back home.

Stupid, of course. They spoke twice a day, sometimes more, and texted copiously. Riley *knew* Christian was coming home but his brain wouldn't turn off the doubts and what-ifs. He'd kept himself busy since Christian left, hoping to keep his mind occupied. He started a new job, hired a new manager for Warm Glow, hosted his parents for a brief visit in mid-January, made a point of getting together with his former teammates, played a couple of hockey games with his rec league, visited Christian's mom, and even took up a new hobby in an effort to pass the time: he was now embarrassingly addicted to *Pet Rescue Saga*.

Sucking in a lungful of air, he raised his hand to knock.

"Riley?"

Startled, he almost choked on oxygen. A guy a couple of inches shorter than him walked toward him from the elevator. Riley had met him...shit, probably eight years ago or so, when he'd flown to Vancouver to see Christian on one of his very few weekends off during university. Eric had been Christian's roommate at the time.

"Hey, man!" Eric held his hand out for a shake. "It's good to see you. Chris didn't mention you were coming to make the trip with him."

"Yeah, uh..." Riley scratched his temple. "He doesn't know."

"Aw." Eric grinned at him. "He's gonna be so happy to see you. He's been a grouchy bastard since he got back from his Christmas vacation."

Christian was always a bit of a grouchy bastard, but if Eric was pointing it out, then his man must've been even grouchier than normal.

Eric walked right into Christian's apartment as if he owned the place. Riley frowned, not liking that one bit.

"Yo, Chris!" Eric shouted into the barren apartment.

The only signs that someone sort-of lived here were the nails hammered into the walls where pictures or art must've once hung and the boxes stacked next to the front door, all neatly labeled. There were less than Riley would've thought, but he knew that Christian had decided to sell the nonessentials: rugs, dishes, pots and pans, his couch, TV, and bed. Riley already had everything at his place. All Christian needed was himself, his clothes, and his personal items.

There was one fairly large box with Riley's name on it, but he didn't have a chance to wonder further before Eric yelled, "You have a visitor."

"If it's my landlord again," came Christian's muffled response from a bedroom to the left, "tell him I've already taken care of everything."

Riley's stomach did something funny at Christian's rumbly voice.

"It's not your landlord," Eric said, hopping up onto the kitchen island.

"Did you bring food?" was Christian's reply.

"Was I supposed to?"

A sigh from the bedroom.

"You know," Eric said to Riley. "I'm almost glad you're taking the grouchy fucker off my hands."

Riley could tell he didn't mean it. He was smiling, but his eyes were sad.

"Please, you know you'll miss me." Christian emerged from the bedroom in old sweats, a T-shirt, and the T necklace Riley had gifted him for Christmas. He held an anorexic roll of packing tape and scissors. Riley's heart jumped into his throat when his boyfriend's icy blue eyes latched onto his.

Christian froze. Riley's doubts doubled. Then Christian's

face went through a series of expressions that had Riley's worries finally fizzing to a quick death: surprise, disbelief, shock, amazement, gratitude, and then, to Riley's delight, excited pleasure.

"Riles," Christian whispered. He thrust the tape and scissors at Eric, then headed for Riley at a clipped pace.

Pulse racing, Riley dropped his backpack and met Christian halfway. Christian's hands framed Riley's face and his lips took possession of Riley's, gently, as if reacquainting himself.

God, the feel of Christian under Riley's hands, the smell of him, the taste... Riley's senses overloaded and he let out a sobbing breath and deepened the kiss.

The past four weeks had been torture, thrusting him back in time to his college years. Him in Denver; Christian here, in Vancouver. Constant texting and phone calls and planning short visits around their busy schedules. Doing the long-distance thing until Christian broke up with him because he couldn't handle the separation anymore.

Not that they'd really been doing a long-distance thing this time around. It was *temporary*, only temporary, while Christian packed up his stuff for the move. Sure, try telling Riley's insecurities that. If he'd constantly worried over the past thirty-two days that Christian was going to change his mind and break up with him, well, it wasn't his fault.

But now he was here, in Christian's arms. Christian smelled so good and tasted so good. Riley gave up any pretense at a civilized hello kiss and attacked Christian's mouth. Christian groaned and wrapped his arms around him, inserting a muscled thigh between Riley's. Riley's dick thickened in his jeans. Inevitable given the past few weeks of nothing but his own hand and phone sex.

"Jesus," Eric muttered from his perch on the counter. "Get a room, guys."

They ignored him.

Christian's lips were soft yet insistent against his, his tongue firm and wet in his mouth. Riley made a throaty sound deep in his chest that had Christian squeezing his ass and driving their semis together. He kept running his hands over Christian's back, his shoulders, up into his hair, reacquainting himself with his boyfriend.

Riley felt like he could finally think again.

There was a thump when Eric jumped off the counter. "I'm going to wait outside. Don't take too long."

The door closed behind him.

Christian pulled back, only to place a quick kiss on Riley's lips.

"Hey, T," Riley said.

Christian chuckled. "Hi." He pecked another fast kiss on Riley's lips. "What are you doing here? Actually, you know what?" He brought Riley in for a hug. "I don't even care. I'm just so fucking glad to see you." His breath whispered against Riley's neck, making him shiver. "I missed you so fucking much."

Riley buried his own face in Christian's neck and inhaled sharply. "I missed you, too." He slipped one hand under Christian's T-shirt to run a hand over bare skin. "I thought you might like company on your drive east."

"Yeah?" Christian dropped tiny kisses along Riley's jaw. Riley sighed in bliss and ran his fingernails along Christian's spine. His man shuddered, pulling back the barest inch, enough so that they could see each other. "What about work?"

"I took a couple days off," Riley said. His hands wandered over Christian's chest, his sides, his stomach.

Christian's abs tightened against his touch even as his eyes darkened with concern. "Is that a good idea?" he asked. "You only started working there two weeks ago. I'm surprised they gave you the time off so soon."

Riley shrugged. "There's no practice today or tomorrow. I'm only missing two practices and the game on Thursday night."

"You might make Thursday's game," Christian said.

"Maybe if we leave early tomorrow. But I already told them I wouldn't be there, so…" He shrugged again. "I'll be back bright and early for Friday morning practice."

Christian's eyes seemed to glitter and he ran his knuckles over the scruff Riley hadn't bothered to shave this morning. "I missed this face," he whispered to himself.

The joy Christian's words produced made Riley feel like he was flying. He closed the inches between them and kissed Christian again, softly, just lips on lips.

When he pulled back, Christian said, "Had I known you were coming, we could've left today. But I promised Eric a last night hanging out before I leave."

"That's okay. Oddly, now that I'm here, the urgency to have you home has faded." Christian grinned at Riley's words. "I'm sorry I'm intruding on your night."

"Don't be." Christian kissed his temple. He couldn't seem to stop kissing Riley. Not that Riley minded. In fact, had Eric not been here, Riley would've dragged Christian straight to the sleeping bag Riley knew he was using as a bed since he'd sold his bed frame and mattress last week.

"Where are you guys headed?" Riley asked, wondering if he'd be invited (of course he would, who was he kidding?) and whether or not he'd be suitably dressed in jeans and a T-shirt seeing as those were all he'd brought with him in addition to a toothbrush.

"Nowhere." Christian jerked his head to an open box against the wall. "We're staying here."

Riley finally released Christian to peer into the box, and couldn't help but laugh. "You're staying in to play board games instead of going out and getting rip roaring drunk?"

"Yup." Christian took a game called *Name 5* out of the box. "I don't want to be hungover tomorrow and Eric doesn't drink. We'll probably play this one. Last time Eric couldn't name five dog breeds."

"Who doesn't know five dog breeds?"

"In my defense," came a voice from the other side of Christian's closed apartment door, "I'm more of a cat person."

Christian told his friend to come in. Riley watched them argue about whether or not Christian had told Eric to bring food, and breathed easily for the first time in thirty-two days.

Watching his man coach hockey was hot as fucking hell, but holy shit, Christian was tired.

"Fuck," he groaned into the couch cushion. "Why am I so tired?"

He'd fallen face-first onto Riley's couch as soon as they'd finished unloading the truck and hadn't moved since.

"Because we've been driving since Monday." Riley's voice came from above him. "Anyone would be tired after four days of driving. Here."

Christian rolled his head and saw Riley holding out a sweating beer bottle. He almost salivated.

"God, I love you," he said, sitting up to take the bottle. "And not just for the beer."

Riley chuckled and sat next to him, feet on the coffee table.

The brew was cold and refreshing after a long few days hauling his crap across the country. Having Riley as company had made the trip infinitely more fun, but it had still been long, especially since he'd done most of the driving. Riley could only drive for so long before his old knee injury made itself known.

"Why do I feel like twice run over roadkill," Christian said, "and you look spry as a fucking daisy?"

Riley tipped his head back and laughed. "I'm not *not* tired," he said. "I'm just..."

He didn't seem able to find a word, so Christian filled it in for him. "High on adrenaline?" He poked Riley's foot with his toe and laid his head on Riley's shoulder. "Your team won tonight." Miraculously, they'd made it on time for the seven o'clock game. Of course, it meant that it was almost ten by the time the game ended and Riley was free to leave. Then the twenty-minute drive home and unloading the truck in the dark, in weather that froze their fingers and toes. It was now almost midnight and Christian was wrecked.

"Yeah," Riley said. Christian could hear the grin in his voice. "I can't take any credit for that, though. I've only been on the coaching staff for two weeks."

"Your goalie's already playing better, though," Christian told him.

"You think?"

"Definitely."

"I thought I was just seeing what I wanted to see."

"Compare tape from tonight's game with one from last month," Christian said. "You'll see."

They sat together for a few minutes, relaxing, eyeing Christian's boxes next to the fireplace. Riley eventually maneuvered them so that he sat with his back in a corner of the couch, Christian resting against him with his back to Riley's chest, feet tangled on the coffee table.

Being here with Riley, in his home—*their* home now—was surreal. He felt the stress of quitting his job, packing his belongings, selling his stuff, renting his apartment, just...fall away. It was crazy how everything they'd been through since they'd met in second grade had brought them here, to this point. Together again, still madly in love but still best friends too, sexual chemistry off the charts.

Speaking of sexual chemistry... Riley was warm and solid behind him and he felt lust pool in his belly. He wasn't *that* tired that he didn't want to christen his new home. He set his beer on the table, but a deep sigh from Riley and what felt like an unclenching of every muscle in Riley's body had Christian pausing.

"You were worried," he realized.

Riley snorted an unamused laugh. "Seems stupid now."

"It's not stupid," Christian protested. Riley's left arm was around his shoulders, his hand resting on Christian's chest. Christian raised his palm to his lips for a kiss. "I'm sorry I didn't realize."

"It is stupid," Riley argued. "I mean there was this part of me I couldn't shut off that was afraid you'd break up with me again, but at the same time I knew you wouldn't. So, see? Stupid."

Christian's heart squeezed for him. "I wish you would've told me."

"No. 'Cause like I said: stupid."

Christian smiled and placed a second kiss on Riley's palm. "Okay, I get it. You're stupid."

"*I'm* not stupid," Riley corrected. "My thoughts are stupid."

"Same damn thing."

"Is not."

"Is too."

"Fuck you."

"Fuck you, too," Christian said cheerfully, matching Riley's tone. Behind him, Riley's chest shook with laughter.

"Hey, what's in that box marked 'crack whore'?" Riley pointed with his foot.

"My bong."

"Your...*what?*" Riley sounded shocked and insulted and faintly horrified.

Christian patted his leg. "Don't worry, I never used it." He'd played hockey in the same leagues as Riley until university. Even as kids they'd known drugs could seriously fuck them up, and they'd needed to stay in shape, so they'd promised each other early on that they wouldn't put that shit in their bodies. "I have a friend who does glasswork and she did a show once," he explained. "I felt bad leaving without buying anything, so I got a little mini bong."

"Seriously? There wasn't, like, a bowl or a trinket dish or something equally mundane you could buy?"

"Well, I guess I sort of did get a bowl," he quipped.

"Har har," Riley said blandly. "You're such a weirdo." His words were gentled by a kiss to Christian's head.

"I'm weird?" Christian tickled Riley's palm. "Says the French Canadian with the first name *Riley*."

"That's not my fault." Riley trapped Christian's hand against his chest. "I didn't name myself. And I don't think *Christian* is French either."

"It's more French than *Riley*."

Riley released a sound of disbelief. "If you say so." He pointed with his foot again. "Why is there a box with my name on it?"

Damn. So much for hoping Riley wouldn't notice.

"I'll show you tomorrow," he hedged, and hid a cringe when he realized his mistake.

"Oh, you have to tell me now," Riley said, laughing. He tried to get up but Christian pressed his back against him and trapped his legs on the table. "Ooh, you don't want me to see! That means it's gotta be good."

They tussled on the couch for a few minutes. By the time Riley had successfully managed to extract himself from Christian's clutches, Christian was half hard and wishing

Riley would forget about the stupid box. Didn't Riley realize they had a bed to christen? Not that they hadn't had sex in Riley's bed before; they totally, definitely, mind-blowingly had. But now that they lived together it was different. More permanent, more solid.

He stretched himself out on the couch, head pillowed on his bicep, and watched Riley move a couple of boxes out of the way to get to the one with his name on it. Despite obviously wanting to get in there, he looked back at Christian with a raised eyebrow.

Christian's sigh was full of resignation, and he waved a hand at Riley. "Go ahead." Might as well get it over with.

Grinning, Riley sat on the floor with the box between his legs and peeled off the packing tape. The smile on his face went from gleeful to confused when he saw what was inside. He pulled out a rectangular box wrapped in snowman-covered wrapping paper, another with black and white polka dot wrapping, another with a blue-and-green plaid pattern, and yet another with cartoon reindeer.

"They're all wrapped," Riley said. Brow furrowed, he peered into the box, where Christian knew there were at least ten more wrapped boxes. "Why? Who are they for? Are you donating them to a charity or something?"

Christian could go with that excuse and save himself the humiliation that was to come, but he'd never lied to Riley and he wasn't about to start now.

A great sigh escaped him and he heaved himself off the couch to take a seat next to Riley on the floor in front of the fireplace.

"Don't laugh," he warned Riley. "But I, uh…" He cleared his throat. "Look, I'm sure you already know that I missed the hell out of you over the past few years." Riley quit playing with a rip in the snowman wrapping paper and looked at him. "I shouldn't've broken up with you, and… This was just my way of feeling close to you." He realized how pathetic he sounded but Riley already knew what a goner he was over him.

Riley blinked at him, his mouth forming a little 'O' of surprise. "These are...all mine?"

"Seven years, give or take, of Christmas and birthday presents."

Riley looked like he had trouble deciding between crying and ripping into his gifts. He did neither. Instead, he dropped the box he was holding, crawled to Christian, pushed him onto his back, and kissed him.

Christian made a sound of surprise. Then he got with the program and hugged Riley closer. Their tongues danced, their legs tangled. Riley's kiss was slow and sweet and filled with longing. Christian's heart thumped in his chest.

Riley pulled back and stared at him, his heart in his eyes.

"What?" Christian rasped.

But Riley just shook his head. His thumb traced Christian's wet bottom lip, swept over his stubbled jaw, brushed his cheekbone. The amazed look on Riley's face, wide eyes, unsteady breathing, mouth opening and closing without a sound... It almost looked like Riley couldn't believe Christian was actually, finally, here.

Christian understood how he felt. He'd spent every day of the past few weeks—every day since he'd returned to Vancouver after New Year's—wondering if Riley had been a dream, if he'd made up their reunion over Christmas. But no. To his astonished wonder, Riley still loved him too.

"I wanna take you to bed," Riley whispered, thumb still tracing Christian's face.

"I want you to take me to bed," Christian said, his hand finding its way into the back of Riley's jeans.

Riley sat up, and as if Christian was tethered to him, he followed. Yet instead of standing, Riley straddled Christian's lap and kissed him quietly, lazily, like he had all the time in the world. The only sounds in the room were their labored breathing, the scritch of Riley's hands on Christian's shadowed jaw, the *whisp* of Christian's hands flitting over Riley's T-shirt, lifting it up. They broke the kiss only long enough to get the shirt over Riley's head.

"T?" Riley said when he pulled back, voice hushed.

The T necklace around Riley's neck caught Christian's attention. His heart melted at the sight of it and he ran his fingers over the worn metal. It didn't even matter anymore what the T stood for. Besides, he had a feeling knowing would make it lose its mysteriousness.

Didn't mean he wouldn't spend the rest of their lives bugging Riley about it, though.

"T?"

Christian placed an open-mouthed kiss on Riley's shoulder and felt Riley's full-body shiver against him.

"Riley, honey?"

Riley framed his face, bringing his head up so their eyes met. Everything Christian felt was reflected back at him in Riley's eyes: acceptance, comfort, hope, adoration, love. He squeezed Riley tighter, wanting him even closer.

Riley's eyes were glassy and when he spoke next, Christian had to blink the wetness out of his own eyes and swallow past the knot in his throat.

"Welcome home."

Curious about Mitch and Alex? Read their story in *On the Ice*, available wherever books are sold!

DEAR

Thank you for coming along on Christian and Riley's journey.

If you enjoyed the book please consider leaving some stars or a review on Amazon, Goodreads, or your favorite review site. Every review helps!

To keep up-to-date on my new releases, and for early access to cover reveals and teasers as well as weekly and monthly giveaways, join my Facebook Group, Amy Aislin's Readers.

And don't forget that you can find bonus content for all of my books on my website at www.amyaislin.com/bonus-content. Character artwork, teasers, excerpts, and blog posts, all in one place.

ABOUT THE
Author

Amy's lived with her head in the clouds since she first picked up a book as a child, and being fluent in two languages means she's read *a lot* of books! She first picked up a pen on a rainy day in fourth grade when her class had to stay inside for recess. Tales of treasure hunts with her classmates eventually morphed into love stories between men, and she's been writing ever since. She writes evenings and weekends—or whenever she isn't at her full-time day job saving the planet at Canada's largest environmental non-profit.

An unapologetic introvert, Amy reads too much and social-izes too little, with no regrets. She loves connecting with readers. Join her Facebook Group, Amy Aislin's Readers, to stay up-to-date on upcoming releases and for access to early teasers, find her on Instagram and Twitter, or sign up for her newsletter.

www.amyaislin.com

instagram.com/amyaislin

facebook.com/amy.aislin

twitter.com/amy_aislin

bookbub.com/profile/amy-aislin